LAST VOYAGE

by the same author

*

THE DARKENED ROOM
A MIND TO MURDER
THE END OF A SHADOW
PLOT COUNTER-PLOT
MY SEARCH FOR RUTH
LEGACY OF EVIL
THE DEATHLESS AND THE DEAD
THE LADY IN BLACK
LETTER FROM THE DEAD
ONE OF US MUST DIE
THE POISONED WEB
POISON PARSLEY

Last Voyage

*

ANNA CLARKE

THE
COMPANION BOOK CLUB
LONDON AND SYDNEY

THE COMPANION BOOK CLUB

The Club is not a library; all books are the property
of members. There is no entrance fee or any
payment beyond the low Club price of each book.
Details of membership will gladly be sent on
request.

Write to:
The Companion Book Club,
Odhams Books, Rushden, Northants.

Or, in Australia, write to:
The Companion Book Club,
C/- Hamlyn House Books, P.O. Box 252
Dee Why, N.S.W. 2099

*Made and printed in Great Britain
for the Companion Book Club
at The Pitman Press, Bath*
600 872 718
1081/371

Chapter One

THE SKY WAS the brilliant blue of late summer and the cliffs of the Isle of Wight shone in an irregular white line between the sky and the sparkling water. SS *Rutland-shire*, sandbagged and camouflaged, her orange funnels painted a dirty grey, moved slowly up Southampton Water towards the doubtful haven of England at war.

The passengers leant on the rail of the promenade deck or moved restlessly about the ship, in and out of the lounges, up and down to their cabins on the lower decks, making silly jokes, exchanging addresses and telephone numbers, promising to keep in touch while knowing full well that they would almost certainly not meet again. And yet there had been a bond forged between them that would never be entirely forgotten. They had been shut up together in this floating prison for three weeks, the five-hundred-odd people on this ship, first-class passengers, cabin-class passengers, and crew, zigzagging over the southern oceans to avoid the German U-boats, unarmed, unprotected by any accompanying warships, never knowing at any moment whether that moment might not be their last. It was a voyage that they would all remember, whatever the

5

fortunes of war might bring to them once they had gone their separate ways.

Most of the passengers were British Islanders returning home after holiday or business visits to South Africa, and even the most experienced voyagers amongst them were finding it the strangest and most heart-turning home-coming that they had ever known.

Among the cabin passengers leaning on the rail on the starboard side watching the busy little puffing tugs pull the great liner round into the narrow channel up to Southampton Docks, were a girl of about twenty-two and a man some twelve or more years older. They had both exclaimed, as had everybody else on deck, when the Needles rocks at the tip of the Isle of Wight came into view, and then they had fallen silent for a while.

'That's the pilot's boat,' said the man presently.

The girl made no reply. She was gazing at the low, flat coastline, and it looked as if her thoughts were miles away.

'Penny for them,' said the man.

She started, turned to face him, and then replied: 'I was only thinking that I wish we were sailing into Table Bay.'

'Homesick for Cape sunshine?'

She shook her head. 'Not really. Anyway, England's not doing too badly for weather at the moment. I don't know why I said that. I suppose it's just apprehension. How long is the war going to last, and what's it going to be like, and all the rest of it.'

'I know,' said the man sympathetically.

He had a pleasant and soothing voice that inspired confidence at once, and made one feel that he really did understand. It was the first thing that the girl had noticed about him, and it was a welcome change from the shrill chatter of the family with whom she shared a table at meals, and whom she knew slightly from having met on a previous voyage some years earlier. Soon after leaving Cape Town she had exchanged names and a few brief details with the man standing by her side – Sally Livingstone and Christian Hofmeyr, both South African born – but they had not really got to know each other until the last few days of the voyage. This was probably, thought Sally, her own fault for being somewhat stand-offish. Chris seemed to be a very unobtrusive person, not like most of the men she had met while travelling. Sally Livingstone was tall and fair, with a sunburnt face, and deep blue eyes whose expression changed rapidly and frequently from eagerness to wariness, as if she would have liked to embrace all life with warmth and openness and trust, but had found reason to be more cautious. She had deliberately refrained from becoming friendly with Christian Hofmeyr, or with anybody else for that matter, for two reasons. First, because she was not a good sailor, and preferred to nurse her frequent bouts of seasickness in solitude; and second, because shipboard romances, although notoriously shortlived, could nevertheless be very upsetting, and she was anxious not to get into any emotional involvement just now.

But Chris was so safe and so undemanding that she had relaxed her guard, and during the last few days they had discovered that they were both keen concert-goers, that both liked reading biographies and detective stories more than anything else, and, most important of all, that both had the same kind of sense of humour. Less progress had been made in exchanging details of their personal circumstances, and it was Sally who up till now had been the more forthcoming, informing him that she had been on a long visit to an uncle and aunt in Cape Town who had not wanted her to leave when war seemed imminent, but that with her mother and sister in England she had felt obliged to take the risk of being torpedoed.

'I couldn't bear to think of being separated from Rose for the duration of the war,' she said. 'We're not twins, but we've always been very close. And even more so after Dad died. That was ten years ago, and we were utterly miserable when Mother told us she'd decided we were to come and live in England. Mother was English, you see, and she never really settled in South Africa but always went on referring to England as "home". I used to notice that, even when I was quite a small child. Children do notice things, much more than people realize.'

'They do indeed,' said Christian in his quiet way.

Sally smiled at him gratefully. She was talking rather a lot, she knew, but he seemed to be genuinely interested, and she would most gladly listen to his own confidences in due course if he liked to make them. He had told her that he was a doctor and had knocked about the world a bit, but that he liked England best and hoped to go into partnership with a former colleague. He also hoped eventually to specialize in psychological medicine, which was his own particular interest, and if being a good listener qualified you to be a good doctor for the mind, thought Sally, then Dr Christian Hofmeyr was going to be a very good mental specialist indeed.

'And children feel things, too,' she went on. 'I know I felt it was insulting to my father that Mother would never accept his country as her own. Of course, I didn't put it into those words when I was so young, but that was definitely how I felt. And so did Rose, although she was always a bit more inclined to stand up for Mother than I was. I suppose I'm old-fashioned, but I do think that if you marry a man and go and live in his home then you ought to make it your home too. Don't you think so, Chris?'

The man standing beside her smiled. He had a long face, with dark hair and eyes and skin, and wore heavy horn-rimmed glasses. A rather sombre face, but the smile transformed it and made him look younger and definitely attractive in an unusual sort of way.

'I don't think I'll express an opinion on that one,' he said, leaving Sally wondering whether he had a wife somewhere, although up till now she had taken it for granted that he was either unmarried or widowed. She remained silent for a moment, giving him the chance to contribute his own experiences if he wished to, but since he said nothing more she continued with her own reminiscences.

'Of course, I can understand that Dad's dying so suddenly was a terrible shock to Mother and she wanted to be back with her own people in England, but it was a shock to Rose and me too. And then to be taken away from all our friends and Dad's folk and our school, and uprooted from home – and Mother's people never really liked us because they disapproved of her marriage in the first place – and England seemed so cold and cramped and cheerless, and the kids at school used to make fun of our colonial accent.'

Sally broke off suddenly. 'What a tale of woe,' she said a moment later, in much lighter tones. 'What a catalogue of tiny grievances compared with a world at war!'

'Why should that make any difference?' said Christian. 'People are still people, with their own lives and feelings, whether it's peace or war. And being taken away from familiar surroundings can be a great trauma for a child. It can leave lasting scars.'

He turned to look at her again, not with a smile this time, but closely and searchingly, and Sally had a momentary and rather disconcerting impression that he could see deeply into her mind.

'Oh, it's not as bad as all that,' she cried. 'We got over it, and my mother's brother James actually got quite fond of us, and I've plenty of friends in London. Oh, no. I don't dislike England now, and Rose positively likes it. She'd never go back to Cape Town. But then, she's just got herself engaged to be married, which makes a difference. It was all very sudden and I haven't yet met him. I hope he's good enough for her. I couldn't possibly part with Rose to anybody who wasn't. So you see, Chris, I don't really mind coming back to England at all, and I certainly want to do my bit in fighting Hitler if they'll let me, in some capacity or other. It's just that I suddenly saw Table Mountain in my mind and I couldn't help thinking, will I ever see it again . . .'

Sally's voice tailed away.

'I know,' said Christian, putting a hand over hers as it lay on the rail. 'It's these arrivals and departures. They always encourage nostalgia. Shall I tell you how England looked to me when I first saw it? Or rather' – and he laughed – 'when I didn't see it. We were on the *Cape Agulhas* – a frightful tumbling old tub – and we'd had a horrible time in the Bay of Biscay as usual. We came up the Channel in thick fog, and the first I saw of England was the inside of a Customs shed. Can you imagine? After leaving the Cape in midsummer. However, I got over it, and, as I say, I'd like to settle in London now.'

10

'It doesn't look as if you'll have much choice,' said Sally. 'I shouldn't think there'll be much travelling going on while the war's on. Unless you go into the forces. Would you join the army?'

'I don't know. I'd like to do my bit, to coin a phrase, but they may be sending only the young medical people and keeping the older ones in civilian work. It all depends how the situation looks when I get to London.'

Again Sally thought he was going to say some more about himself, but again he seemed to think better of it, and they fell silent once more. It was not an awkward silence, but rather a peaceful and companionable one. It was like the silences that Sally remembered from the times when her father used to take her round the botanical gardens at Kirstenbosch, and they would suddenly stop still, the tall fair man and the little fair girl, and look in speechless joy, and wonder at the great flaming bushes of proteas in front of them for a few minutes before walking on in silence again.

Perhaps it was this moving memory that loosened Sally's mind and led her to open her heart to the man beside her as she had never done to anyone in her life before.

'You were talking about childhood trauma and your first voyage to England,' she said. 'My first voyage was a terrible one, too. Not only because of Dad's death and because I was ill and homesick, but for a very special reason. There was something that happened on that voyage, something that nobody knew about but myself. And one other person.' Her voice dropped almost to a whisper. 'Perhaps that's what coloured my first impressions of England, that I couldn't get over the horror of it. I was only eleven, you see. I had nightmares about it for years. In fact, it's still with me now, if I let myself think.'

Sally shivered suddenly in the sunshine. People around them on the deck were beginning to bustle about and ask each other whether they were sure they had got their passports. Others went down to their cabins to check yet again that their packing was done. Crewmen began to position themselves for throwing the line, preparatory to securing the ship with the great hawsers. In fifteen minutes' time, unless some sudden disaster dropped from the skies, SS *Rutlandshire* would have brought her precious cargo of human lives safely into harbour.

Sally Livingstone gripped the rail with both hands and stared into the calm water many feet below. It hypnotized her, drew her towards it, as water looked on from a great height always did. Even from a lesser height it was nearly as bad. Before her long visit to Cape Town she had occasionally gone out for the evening with a medical student who was a regular customer at the bookshop where she worked. They would have a meal in a Lyons Corner House and then walk down to the river, because he liked to lean on the parapet of Westminster Bridge and quote Wordsworth to her to show that he was not totally ignorant of literature.

These moments were always an agony to Sally. She would stand on the pavement with her back to the parapet and look across the road at the view in the opposite direction, concentrating on the lights in the Houses of Parliament, and on the clock face of Big Ben as if they were a sort of talisman, a symbol of lasting safety. If Charles went on rhapsodizing for too long she would turn her head quickly to the left and stare at the serrated

12

outline of St Thomas's Hospital, its separate blocks showing up on the southern banks of the Thames like some great castle turret.

Charles had never known that she had this horror of looking down on water from above. Neither had Rose, nor her mother, nor anybody else. It was not too difficult to hide, even on a boat, because as long as she did not actually look over the edge she was perfectly all right. Walking round the decks, playing deck tennis or quoits, climbing the companionway to the upper levels – these, and plenty of other things, she could happily do. It was the direct pull of the water on the eyes, whether the water was frothing and turbulent or calm and softly rippling, that held the fatal fascination for her.

Sally had more or less resigned herself to living with it for the rest of her life, and with the underlying horror, too. Once or twice when she had been working at the bookshop she had come across a book dealing with the wonders of modern psychology and the amazing cures that had been achieved by helping people to bring to light the memory of something that had frightened them. On these occasions she had thought of asking Charles Brent whether he knew of anybody who was practising psychoanalysis, but had never actually done so, making the excuse to herself that although she liked Charles well enough, she didn't really want to tell him about something so very personal that he probably wouldn't understand in any case, because he was a practical and unimaginative sort of person who would no doubt be very good at dealing with broken ankles and getting children through the measles, but for whom the oddities of the human mind were a closed book. In her more honest moments, however, Sally admitted to herself that the reason she had never done anything about seeking relief for this deep, secret fear of hers was that she was too afraid of uncovering it.

This made it all the more extraordinary that she should be talking about it at last not to Charles, whose parents she knew and whose life was as open as daylight, but to this dark stranger, about whom she knew nothing except what he had told her. Christian Hofmeyr seemed to have a strangely soothing effect on her. Here she had been for more than half an hour actually leaning on the rail of the ship, looking at the shore-line rather than looking down, admittedly, but nevertheless leaning on the rail. And there had up till now been none of the usual stabbing panic, nothing but a distant rumble of apprehension that was not intolerable.

Perhaps after all it was not so extraordinary that she was going to tell her story to Chris. Had not her Uncle James once said, in a rare burst of insight, that the best person to tell your worst troubles to was a sympathetic stranger? Relatives were impossible, and friends were too unreliable. And after all, Chris had said he was trained in psychiatry, and apart from that Sally had a feeling that he was not an entire stranger, but that in some way or other their lives were already linked together. Perhaps this was just imagination; perhaps it was wishful thinking, a hope that in some way their lives would become linked in the future, because there was no doubt that she felt very attracted to him. At any rate, she had not the slightest doubt now that he would understand.

As if determined to test her trust in him to the utmost, Sally deliberately forced herself to lean far over the rail

14

and look straight down at the water that the great liner was gently cleaving. Giddiness overtook her, and she felt as if she were tipping up and falling. An arm came round her and pulled her a little away from the rail. Sally rubbed her eyes and shook herself as if coming out of a nightmare.

'That's my phobia,' she said smiling and trying to speak lightly. 'Looking down on water. When you're practising as a psychoanalyst you must try to cure me of it.'

'Perhaps we can do something about it before that very questionable date. Do you feel like telling me what happened on that ship?'

'I don't really know. Or rather, I do know, very well indeed. But I'm not sure whether it really happened. Sorry. That sounds idiotic. What I'm trying to say is that although it's perfectly clear in my mind, I sometimes wonder whether I was seeing things that weren't there. Having hallucinations, I mean.'

'You don't strike me as the sort of person to have hallucinations,' said Christian, looking at her keenly through the heavy spectacles. 'You strike me as very sane and well-balanced. That's a great compliment, coming from a budding psychiatrist,' he added, once more producing the sudden smile that transformed his whole face.

'I was very weak at the time,' said Sally, flushing slightly. 'I'd been terribly seasick.'

'That could make a difference,' he admitted. 'It's true that impressions during illness can be very vivid, but they can also be very unreliable.'

'And I've got a vivid imagination at the best of times,' said Sally. 'It used to get me into trouble sometimes when

I was a kid. I wish I could be sure that I'd imagined this. Or that I knew it was only a nightmare, and could forget. But I can't forget it, because I know in my heart that I didn't imagine it. It's quite different from the sort of day-dreams I sometimes have, or the sort of stories I used to make up and that got me into trouble. It's something that really happened. I know it is. Perhaps after all I'd better not tell you. It could be dangerous.'

'That isn't likely to deter you. After all, the whole of life is going to be dangerous now.'

'Yes, you're right. I'm being silly, and I know you'll never mention it to anyone else. But apart from my own nightmares about it I've always had this fear that if by any chance I were ever to run into him again . . . You see, Chris, I'm sure I'd recognize him. I actually saw the man's face.'

'The face of this man who assaulted you on the boat? I take it that it was some sort of sexual assault?'

It was spoken in a calm, almost clinical tone of voice, just the sort of voice that Sally needed to hear to give her the strength to go on.

'Oh no,' she said. 'It was nothing like that. He saw me, but he never came near me. I'd got back into the cabin and shot the bolt by the time he came out of the bathroom. Oh no. There's no rape involved. Not that I know of, anyway. But I did see him killing someone. At least, I think I did. And he knew that I saw him.'

Chapter Two

'GANGWAY ON B Deck! Have your passports ready in the saloon . . . Gangway on B Deck . . .'

The loud voice of authority broke into the silence that had followed Sally's last words.

'Damn,' said Christian, 'what a moment to choose. I suppose we'll have to go down, although I'm sure it will be hours before we're allowed to land. The immigration people are going to be slower than ever in war-time. Checking for German spies, no doubt. Do you think we've got any spies on board, Sally? Personally I rather fancy that little man with a beard and blue beret who's always trotting round the deck first thing in the morning.'

Sally tried to smile, but it was not easy. It had shaken and weakened her to speak of the fear that had been locked away in her mind for so long, and she would have liked now to be quietly alone for a while and let the worst of the quickened memory die down again. But there was no chance of this, and she felt grateful to Chris for bringing her gently back into the present reality instead of instantly commenting on her story. He was behaving perfectly, and she had been quite right to trust him.

'Spies,' she said as brightly as she could. 'Well, I think it's the mother of those awful kids. It's always the least likely person, and you can hardly imagine anyone more unlikely.'

'Perhaps it's us. Are you a spy, Sally?'

'I don't think so. Are you?'

'Of course I am. Can't you see that I'm wearing a wig and that my spectacles are only a disguise?'

Sally put up a hand and tugged at his hair.

'Ouch!' cried Christian.

'Serves you right,' said Sally, and ran across to the other side of the ship.

SS *Rutlandshire* was now alongside the quay, where a small group of people waited with strained and anxious faces for the first glimpse of friends and relatives they had come to meet.

'I'm not expecting anyone,' said Christian. 'Most of my friends are medical people who'll be too busy to get away. Will your mother and sister be here?'

'I doubt it,' replied Sally. 'Mother definitely wouldn't come. Rose is only doing odd typing jobs for an agency, so she'd get the time off, but she probably won't want to leave Mother.'

'Is your mother an invalid, then?'

'No,' replied Sally shortly, 'but Rose worries about her.'

'Say no more. Those words tell volumes. I can see it all. If neither of us is being met, then how about going on the boat-train together? If there is a boat-train, that is. We'll probably find the whole country in total chaos.'

'Southampton's still there, anyway,' said Sally, glancing at the line of Customs sheds and the great cranes and factory chimneys beyond. 'It's not yet been razed to the ground.'

'Don't speak too soon. It may well happen. It'll be a prime target for bombing. All the big ports will.'

'All the big ports,' repeated Sally. 'And the little ones too. And all the cities, and the railways, and the factories, and the bridges . . .' She stood for a moment looking very thoughtful. 'Doesn't it make you realize, coming from Africa, just what a tiny island this is? A crowded and defenceless little island.'

'Whose people have conquered the world.'

'The Empire on which the sun never sets. Our ancestors did some pretty horrible things when acquiring it. At least, mine did. Including some nasty things to your ancestors in South Africa.'

'I'm only half Afrikaner, Sally,' said Christian.

'And I'm one quarter,' she replied. 'We're all mongrels, aren't we? It's so utterly *silly*, apart from everything else, this Nazi race business. Come on, Chris. Let's go and join that queue. I don't really want to be docking in Table Bay, you know,' she added as they made their way down to the saloon. 'If England's good enough for you, it's good enough for me. Thank you for letting me talk.'

'Thank you for confiding in me. If you'd like to tell me more about it I think you'll find it will relieve the phobia, but we will need some peace and quiet.'

'And there won't be much of that on the boat-train.'

'Would you like me to phone you tomorrow morning and fix a time to meet?'

'If you don't mind,' said Sally, 'I'd rather ring you. The phone's in the hall in our flat in Park Mansions. I'm not being secretive, and I'd like you to meet my mother and sister some time, but . . . well, you know what families are.'

19

Christian smiled. 'Yes. I know what families are. All right, then. You get in touch with me. But don't leave it too long. Once you manage a breakthrough in a case like yours it's as well to follow it up as soon as possible.'

'You do look on me as a patient, then?'

'If you wish.'

'Not as a friend?'

'As a friend too, if you wish.'

What Sally was actually wishing was that he would stop behaving so perfectly, if only for a moment or two, and behave more like most of the men she had known. It was very difficult to tell whether he was interested in her for her own sake, or only interested in her as a case of phobia due to a childhood trauma. That she herself was now very interested in him indeed was beyond all doubt, and she very much wished she knew more about him. However, at least they were to meet again, and no doubt she would find some way of making the relationship rather less one-sided.

The boat-train, on which they found seats at last after a long wait at the Customs, was not conducive either to close confidences or to a pleasant furthering of an acquaintance. Darkness had fallen. The lights in the compartment were dim and the blinds were drawn tightly over the windows. The atmosphere was stale and stuffy, thick with smoke and with the doubts and fears of worried and apprehensive people.

'If we don't all die of bombs we're going to die of claustrophobia,' said Sally after a while. 'At the moment I feel as if I'd give ten years of my life for one breath of fresh air.'

'Cheer up,' said Christian. 'It's not for very long.'

'Tell me about your London flat,' said Sally, determined, despite her discomfort, to try to find out more about him. 'Near Albany Street, didn't you say?'

'That's right. The wrong side of the park. Not like you people on the posh side. There's not really much to tell. It's a converted terrace house, and I've got the first floor. It's adequately furnished, and there's room for my books and a few other things I haven't wanted to part with. There's a nervous elderly lady on the ground floor, who, I imagine, will have fled from London at the outbreak of war, and a middle-aged couple in the top flat who are friendly but not obtrusive. I'm depending on them to let me have a little milk and bread tonight to supplement my stock of tins in the store cupboard, since I've no other provisions.'

This was, thought Sally, about the longest consecutive speech that she had heard Christian make, but when it was over she still didn't feel that she had made much headway in getting to know him.

'When will you be starting work?' she asked.

'It depends. If my colleague wants me to join the practice at once, then it will be straight away. If not, then I'll have to see if they can do with me in any of the hospitals for a while.'

Sally noted that he did not seem to be worried about money. Perhaps he had private means, or had a lot saved up. After all, even a flat on the wrong side of the park cost something to rent, and he had spent at least three months, presumably without being paid, on the visit to South Africa.

'I should think doctors of all people are going to be very much in demand,' she said.

21

'If we come under heavy air attack they certainly will be,' he agreed. 'But that doesn't seem to have happened yet.'

'Do you think it will happen?'

'I've no idea,' said Christian.

He sounded uninterested, and Sally suddenly felt very depressed. On the boat there had been a strong sense of comradeship, of shared adventure, of facing danger together, but on this horrible train journey there was no such feeling; nothing but the sense of a lot of separate individuals all shut up in their own frustrations and worries. Even the man to whom she had entrusted her own secret seemed very distant from her, although actually they were seated side by side. She made a few more remarks and then gave up. Perhaps he was just tired. After all, it had been a most exhausting day, and she was feeling very sleepy herself. Her eyes closed, and it seemed only seconds later that the train jerked to a halt.

'Are we there?' asked Sally.

Christian leaned across her and pulled the blind aside a fraction so that he could peer out.

'You oughtn't to do that,' said a military-looking elderly man very severely. 'Mustn't show a light. Could endanger the whole train.'

'But there isn't a raid on,' protested Sally.

'That's nothing to do with it. Rules are made to be kept. Discipline. That's what this country needs, and it's going to get it now.'

The military-looking man glared at the other occupants of the compartment and then shook out his newspaper and proceeded to glare at that in the dim light. Sally and Christian and the five other people all made sympathetic

22

faces at each other and in a few minutes the train moved on.

Waterloo Station was a gloomy chaos. As they came through the ticket barrier Sally found herself anxiously scanning the waiting faces beyond. That her mother would be there to meet her she neither wished for nor expected, but she could not help hoping that Rose might have come, either alone or with the new fiancé. Sally was beginning to feel badly in need of the sight of a familiar face to welcome her to this dark and rather frightening city that felt so different from when she had left it six months before. Surely it would have been possible for them to find out from the shipping offices which boats were safely in? Other passengers on the *Rutlandshire* had been met at Southampton, so news must have got through. And surely they must know she was coming, because she had cabled from Cape Town that in spite of the war clouds gathering she was determined to sail.

'No sign of them?'

Christian at her side sounded once again the sympathetic man to whom she had talked on the boat, and Sally told herself that she must have imagined that feeling of distance, even of indifference, that she had felt in him on the train. It was so easy to imagine things when one was tired and worried.

'I can't see anyone,' replied Sally.

All around them people were greeting each other and clinging together in the relief of reunion. Sally felt more desolate every minute. 'I think I'd better telephone,' she said, 'rather than just turn up. They may not even be there. Mother's very nervous. They may have gone to stay with Uncle James in Oxford.'

Christian offered to wait with the luggage while Sally joined one of the queues outside the public telephone booths. When at last one fell vacant she found that a coin had become jammed and it was impossible to use. The thought of joining another queue and waiting round again, possibly with the same result, was more than she could bear, and she felt very near to tears when she rejoined Christian by the luggage.

'I'll just have to get a taxi and risk it,' she said. 'If there's no one there I'll have to go to a hotel. I haven't a door key with me and there's no night porter.'

Christian replied in his quiet and kindly way. 'We'll share the taxi, since we're going in the same direction. I shall leave you at Park Mansions if all is well, and you will give me a ring tomorrow. If there's nobody there, then you can come and sleep in my flat. It's perfectly respectable.' The smile came and went quickly. 'I've got two rooms. You can phone your uncle and we can both have something to eat, which is becoming rather urgent, I feel.'

Sally would not have had the spirit to refuse even if she had wished to do so. She thanked him, and they joined the queue for taxis. It moved very slowly, and every now and then they looked at each other despairingly.

'What did you do in the Great War, Daddy?' said Christian at one point.

'I stood in the blackout in a queue,' said Sally and they both laughed.

It was nearly eleven when their turn came at last.

'I suppose we'll get used to it,' said Sally as they drove with shaded headlights through darkened streets. 'I wish it was spring, though, and not autumn, so that we could look forward to more daylight soon.'

When they came to the road encircling Regent's Park she fell silent, staring out of the window for some sign of familiar places. A glimmer of light she identified as the entrance to the Zoo, and a few minutes later the taxi crossed the road and drew up at the entrance to a big block of flats. Sally wound down the window and peered out.

'Our flat's on the ground floor,' she said. 'I can't see any lights in the windows.'

Her voice was flat with disappointment.

'You're not supposed to see any lights in the windows,' said Christian. 'They'd be breaking the law if you did.'

'Oh yes. Of course. What an idiot I am! I'll go and see if anyone's there before we get out my things.'

Within half a minute she was back. 'I didn't need to ring,' she said. 'I can see the hall light on through the glass in the front door and I can hear them talking.'

'Right,' said Christian pulling her two big suitcases out of the taxi. 'Where do you want me to put them?'

'In the foyer. To the left. It's number three.'

He put down the suitcases and said, 'Good night and good luck.'

'Good night,' said Sally. 'And thanks. Thanks for everything.'

Now that the moment had come to part she felt very reluctant to see him go. It was as if they had lived through whole lifetimes of experience together, as if it was this dark stranger of whom she knew so little who was an essential part of her life, and not the people who were behind the glazed front door of the flat.

'That's all right,' he said. 'Don't leave it too long to come and tell me about that business that's worrying you.'

'I won't leave it long,' she promised.

He turned at the main entrance to the block, and smiled and waved at her, and she waited until she heard the taxi drive away before putting her finger to the bell of No. 3. She had an extraordinary sense of having been at a very vital turning point in her life, but whether she had missed a great opportunity or escaped a great danger she could not tell.

Chapter Three

AFTER SALLY HAD rung the bell she heard sounds of movement in the flat, and her mother's voice, with its low whine raised a tone or two, saying: 'Whoever can that be at this hour? It can't be Rose because she has her key. Is it the air-raid warden? We're not showing any light, are we, James?'

'Course we aren't.' The abrupt male voice brought some relief to Sally's ears. If Mother were here alone I don't believe she would even let me in, thought the girl.

Footsteps came towards the door, and a dim shape was just discernible through the frosted glass.

'Don't worry, Sarah,' said Uncle James's voice. 'I'll deal with him if it's the warden. Little jumped-up jacks-in-office. Petty Hitlers.'

The door was pulled open, and for a moment Sally's Uncle James stood there speechless. He was a tall man with iron-grey hair, in appearance not unlike the military-looking man who had been in the compartment on the train. But, as Sally and Rose had soon found out, his bark was worse than his bite, and much of the gruffness and bluster was due to shyness.

'Well I never! Look who's here! Just look who's here!' He held out both arms to her, and it was all Sally could do to keep back the tears as she kissed him. The strain of the long and dangerous voyage, the arrival in this dark and apprehensive city, the sense of being personally unwelcomed and unloved, had so worn her down that her vitality was at its lowest ebb, and the little gesture of kindness from her uncle was almost too much for her. But her mother's reaction soon stiffened her resistance again.

'Sally!' screamed Mrs Livingstone, more as if she had seen a ghost than a living daughter. 'What on earth are you doing here ? Why aren't you in Cape Town?'

'Because the *Rutlandshire* left on schedule although a lot of the passengers cancelled. Didn't you get my cable?'

'Cable? How can I remember what cables we've had, with everything turned upside down and not knowing what was happening from one moment to the next!'

A typical reaction, thought Sally, in the coldly dispassionate way in which she always regarded her mother. The war was looked on purely as a nuisance designed to cause annoyance to Sarah Livingstone.

Sally's mother was tall and fair, and had once been a great beauty, a true English rose to the rather rough diamond of a businessman whom she had married. She would have been a beauty still if it had not been for the aura of bitterness and resentment that covered her like a thick varnish, isolating her from any true contact with any other human being.

'I don't know where you're going to sleep,' she went on after giving Sally a token peck on the cheek. 'Your uncle is in your room and we weren't expecting to have to start making up beds at this time of night.'

'I'll go in with Rose,' and 'I'll doss down on the drawing-room sofa,' said Sally and her uncle, speaking simultaneously.

Mrs Livingstone did not look at all pleased at being thus presented with two solutions to the problem.

'I suppose they're all congratulating themselves in Cape Town,' she said while Uncle James was bringing in Sally's suitcases, 'at being a nice long way away from all the troubles in Europe.'

'I never heard any mention of it,' said Sally coolly. 'Most of our cousins are volunteering for the air force.' A moment later she said in a more friendly manner; 'I've got some presents for you and Rose. Would you like to see them now or shall we wait till tomorrow?'

'Jewellery, I suppose,' said Sarah Livingstone putting a hand to her mouth to half-stifle a yawn. 'Very kind of them, no doubt, but somewhat lacking in imagination. We are not likely to be attending many social functions in the immediate future.'

'I'll wait till the morning then,' said Sally with a sort of desperate calmness that was followed by a minor explosion. 'I suppose I may make myself some tea,' she cried, anger and contempt showing clearly in her voice, 'since I've had nothing to eat or drink since noon. Or would that be too disturbing for you?'

Sarah Livingstone burst into tears, ran into her bedroom, and slammed the door. Uncle James put down Sally's suitcases in the hall and took the girl by the arm.

'Come on, Sal,' he said, drawing her along the passage to the kitchen at the back of the flat. 'We'll have a cup together. I'll put the kettle on while you have a bit of a wash. Dirty business, travelling. Specially in war-time.

Train I came up to town in this morning was filthy. Quite unnecessary. Just slackness. War's going to be made the excuse for slackness all round, if you ask me.'

Sally took no notice of this familiar bumbling. It was no more than a superficial habit with Uncle James, a way of filling in moments of emotion with which he did not know how to deal. It was in quite a different category from her mother's festering bitterness that came from deep within.

'There you are, my gal,' he said ten minutes later, as he put a plate of bacon and eggs in front of her. 'You'll have to pretend it's breakfast time. It's the only thing I know how to cook.'

'It tastes like manna from heaven,' said Sally. 'And as for the tea . . .'

'Mustn't be too hard on your mother,' said Uncle James presently in his very gruffest manner. 'Nerves, y'know. Quite understandable, really. Everyone's nervy. Feel a bit that way myself, as a matter of fact. It's all this waiting about for something to happen. Gets you down.'

'I know,' said Sally. 'I'm sorry.

'And we didn't really expect you. Felt sure you'd turn back when war was declared. It was a shock to your mother, y'know. Matter of fact it gave me quite a turn myself, opening the door and seeing you standing there.'

'I know,' said Sally again. 'I did try to phone but never got through.'

'Damned telephone operators.' He began his ground-bass grumbling again. 'Hopelessly inefficient.'

Sally ate and drank gratefully and made no attempt to come to the defence of the telephone service.

'I'd better not go near Mother,' she said a minute or two later. 'It'll only make her worse. Rose will calm her down. When d'you expect her in, Uncle? It's getting very late.'

James Davenant's red face took on an even deeper colour. 'Too late, if you ask me,' he said. 'But then she's not *my* daughter.'

'Is she out with Frank?' asked Sally with quickening interest.

Uncle James merely grunted.

'I don't suppose she's had much chance to go out with him,' continued Sally, 'with Mother being so nervy. And with you being here it gave her a chance to get away.'

James Davenant made another snorting noise, and Sally read in it intense disapproval.

'Why shouldn't Rose have a night out once?' she said. 'She doesn't get much fun, and after all, she is engaged to be married to him. What's he like, Uncle James? Frank Sedgemore, I mean. I'd never even heard of him till she wrote and told me a few weeks ago. It must have been a whirlwind romance. I hope he's good enough for Rose.' Sally pushed aside her empty plate and looked keenly at her uncle across the kitchen table. 'I don't believe you think he is. What's the matter with him?'

James Davenant shifted uneasily on his chair, rubbed a finger up and down behind his ear, and champed at his iron-grey moustache before replying.

'Matter of fact, I can't stand the feller,' he burst out at last. 'Damn dago-looking type. Says he's English, but I don't believe it.'

Sally was not unduly alarmed by these strictures. She had a pretty clear idea of the standards by which Uncle James assessed his fellow-mortals. They were by no means her own standards, but that did not lessen her

31

affection for him or make her feel any less grateful for his generosity. It was Uncle James's money, partly inherited, partly acquired during his years in the City, that enabled the three women to live in a comfortable flat in a desirable residential area and employ a daily servant. Not that any of this mattered very much to Sally, and she believed that it did not matter to Rose, but to their mother it was all-important. It always hurt the girls to hear her complain that their father had left her so much less well-off than she had expected, and these complaints would have been even worse if it had not been for Uncle James. He was a bachelor, a good many years older than his sister Sarah, and he lived with the older, unmarried sister, Gertrude, in the big house that had belonged to his parents and grandparents. Rose and Sally were the only members of the young generation in the family, and they did their best to play the part of charming devoted nieces for his sake. At least, Sally had to play a part: to Rose it came naturally.

For James Davenant a 'dago-type' could mean anything from a rather dark-skinned Frenchman to an Egyptian or a Persian. It could also mean an upper-class English Jew if his colouring was sufficiently noticeable. In fact, thought Sally as her uncle was speaking, it could even mean a South African doctor of European ancestry if he happened to have the sort of dark hair and swarthy skin that Christian Hofmeyr had. So it would need a lot more evidence than this against Rose's fiancé for Sally to disapprove of the engagement.

'What does Frank do?' she asked. 'Rose never told me when she wrote.'

Uncle James snorted again. 'Runs some sort of an

agency,' he said contemptuously. 'An agent! Now that's not a name anyone would give to themselves if they had a decent profession or honest trade. There's something deuced fishy about it, Sal, when a man has to put himself down as an agent. You mark my words.'

This time Sally did not feel inclined to smile. Even allowing for Uncles James's viewpoint on the world, there was still something disturbing in what he said. She herself would have been much more pleased to hear that Rose's fiancé was a doctor or lawyer, a schoolteacher or a parson, or even a butcher or a greengrocer.

'What sort of an agency does Frank run?' she asked.

'Typing, clerking; office services, I believe they call it. Some grand name or other. Whole thing's a piece of confidence trickery if you ask me. It's one of these new-fangled American ideas. You don't hire a clerk or a book-keeper to come and sit in your office and do your work in an honest way. You get this agent to find somebody for you and pay him a percentage.'

'But why not?' said Sally veering round to a feeling of reassurance again. 'They're doing that more and more nowadays. It's only a matter of convenience. There's nothing fishy about it at all. If a firm wants somebody for only a few weeks it makes sense to get them in temporarily from an agency instead of taking them on as permanent staff. I suppose it is Frank's agency that Rose has been working for. She wrote me she was giving up the job in the shop and going to do odd jobs so that she could spend more time with Mother. Honestly, Uncle James, if that's all you've got against Frank Sedgemore I don't think there's much need to worry about Rose. He's probably a very good businessman, and will make a fortune.'

33

'Not in war-time he won't. Not in any honest way. Business is dead. Only the rogues will thrive. Besides, he's too old for her.'

'Too old?'

'Forty if he's a day.'

'Oh.' Sally digested this. Rose had not said anything about Frank's age. In fact, she had written very little about him except that he was clever and 'man-of-the-worldish', and that she felt safe with him and knew he would look after her. And that she was terribly happy, and dying for him and Sally to meet, and so afraid that if war did break out it would be a long time before the meeting took place.

'Oh,' said Sally again, beginning to adjust her ideas and speaking her conclusions aloud. 'I think what it is, Uncle, is that Rose feels she needs an older man. I do, too, you know, in a way. I suppose it's having lost our father when we were young. Don't you think that's what it is?'

'I dare say it is,' retorted Uncle James, 'but it doesn't make the feller any less of a bounder. Trading on Rose's needs like that.'

'But if he really loves her and if she loves him . . . I mean, why did he ask her to marry him if he doesn't love her? What can he hope to get from Rose?'

'A packet of money when I die, that's what he can hope to get from Rose,' said James Davenant, with a brutal directness quite unlike his usual rumblings.

'Oh, do you think Rose has told him that?'

'No need to, m'dear. He's got other ways of finding out.'

'You mean through Mother?' said Sally, suddenly struck with an unpleasant suspicion.

34

Uncle James cleared his throat loudly. 'M'm. Yes. I wasn't going to mention it, but that's what I do mean. For some reason or other your mother's dead keen on the man.'

Sally questioned him further, but he fussed around her and cleared the table and refused to reply.

'Time you were in bed,' he said several times. 'Good night's sleep, that's what you need now.'

Sally had indeed almost exhausted the second wind that had come with the stimulation of food and the talk with Uncle James.

'I'll get into Rose's bed,' she said. 'She won't mind.'

Uncle James muttered something about going to see how her mother was and left the kitchen too. He had taken a few steps along the passage that led to the front of the flat, and Sally had just gone into Rose's bedroom which was next to the kitchen, when there came the sounds of a key turning in a lock, and of restrained but clearly audible voices, a man's and a woman's.

'They're still up.' It was Rose speaking. 'I hope it doesn't mean Mother's not well.'

'She'll be all right, honey,' the man's voice replied. 'She's not been alone.'

To Sally's ear there was something phoney about the voice, something conceited and complacent, and she felt sure that the slight American accent was assumed. She had a mental picture of a slick salesman, varnished and Brylcreemed, and at the same time wondered guiltily whether she was not prejudiced because of what her uncle had said.

It was Uncle James who spoke next, at his very gruffest, but he was quickly interrupted by Sarah Livingstone, who welcomed Rose and her fiancé with exaggerated cries of delight.

'You're terribly late, you naughty boy,' Sally heard her say, and winced at the archness in her mother's voice. 'Where on earth have you been? I didn't know there was any night life left in London.'

'Ah, you can always find something when you know the ropes,' replied the man's voice.

Uncle James gave one of his snorts, and Sally could guess what he was thinking: this bounder will always know the ropes. She stood just inside the open door of Rose's room, torn between the longing to run and greet her sister, and the equally strong reluctance to have their reunion witnessed by this man whom she had already come to dislike. Rose must then have caught sight of Sally's big suitcases standing near the telephone table, because she gave a loud cry.

'Is Sally here? How wonderful! D'you mean she made the journey after all? Oh, why didn't I know! Why wasn't I here to meet her!'

Sally felt tears sting her eyes, and took her decision. It was not fair to keep Rose waiting another second, Frank or no Frank. She pulled the door open wide, and as she did so she heard Frank's voice.

'I guess this is where I bow out, folks. At such a meeting even fiancés are *de trop*.'

These were the last words that Sally heard. After that it was chaos in her mind. She stepped out of Rose's room and looked down the passage towards the group standing near the front door of the flat. The light was directly above them, and all four faces were turned in her direction. Rose gave another cry and ran towards her. If

Rose's arms had not held her up Sally believed she would have fallen. She had only looked for a moment, but, as on that ocean liner ten years ago, one moment and one look had been enough. She had seen the three faces clearly – her uncle's, her mother's, and the third one. The face of a tall, thin man with thick, smooth black hair and dark eyes. And a dark complexion like a gypsy, with the lighter line of a curious sickle-shaped scar on the left cheek-bone, following the shape of the eye. It was a face Sally had seen before and that she had told Dr Christian Hofmeyr that she would never forget.

The face of the man on the boat.

Chapter Four

'YOU'RE NOT TO talk any more tonight,' said Rose half an hour later. 'I'm going to sleep on the drawing-room sofa because you'll never stop talking if I stay here. I'm dying to hear more about your voyage, but it'll have to wait. And I'm dying to tell you about Frank, but that'll have to wait too. In any case there'll be no need to tell you, because you'll see for yourself. Oh Sally, I'm so happy! You know I've always wanted someone to look after me – I'm such a feeble creature compared with you. I feel really safe with Frank. He can make up his mind quickly, and always knows what to do. And it's so wonderful that Mother likes him. I was so afraid she'd think he was . . .'

'Not out of the top drawer,' said Sally with a great effort.

She had decided, after the first shock, that nothing was to be gained by an immediate revelation to Rose. That was as far as her exhausted mind would go at the moment, and decision involved playing a part, listening without reservation to Rose's enthusiasm, even putting in a suitable comment now and then. To play such a part at this moment was almost beyond her powers, but fortunately Rose seemed to have no suspicion and was very willing to attribute to Sally's weariness any apparent lack of enthusiasm about Frank.

'Not out of the top drawer,' she repeated with a little smile. 'Frank's certainly not that. And proud of it. He was born in India, and his father deserted his mother when he was a child, and they had terrible struggles. But you don't want to hear about that tonight. Now I really am going. Sleep well. I'm so very very glad you're safely home. It was so brave of you to come. I'd never have done it. To think you could have been torpedoed – like the *Athenia*!'

Rose concluded on a little gasp of horror. Sally sat up in bed, and they clung together as they had done as children, with a sort of defiant desperation, the two of them against the world.

'It won't make any difference to us,' said Rose. 'Not even Frank will make any difference. We'll always be the same. Won't we, Sal?' she added pleadingly.

'Always the same,' said Sally with an even greater effort than before. Then she loosed her grip and fell back against the pillow with her eyes closed, conscious, but beyond any further struggle.

Rose leant over and kissed her, switched off the bedside lamp, and tiptoed out of the room. She was an older, gentler, and some people would say prettier version of her sister, her mother's favourite because she was the more malleable. Uncle James secretly preferred her, too, although among his rigid canons of behaviour was one that said the two girls must always be treated exactly the same. But it was Sally, the younger, the bolder and more independent, and also the more difficult and obstinate, whom her father had loved best, and who had mourned him the more deeply.

Rose settled herself comfortably on the soft sofa cushions and lay awake for a little while, thinking about Sally and about her own future, and feeling guilty, for such was her nature, that with all Europe darkened by the black clouds of war she herself should be feeling so happy and hopeful. She had never been in love before. The young men in her mother's circle of acquaintances had all seemed to be so blasé and superior that they frightened her; while those whom she had met in the various jobs she had done had frightened her in a different way – by their crudeness and lack of subtlety.

Frank Sedgemore had appealed to her from their first meeting. He had made her feel beautiful and desirable without making her feel hunted, and he had never sneered at her ignorance of politics and finance, but had treated her as an intelligent and attentive pupil, capable of understanding anything once it was explained to her. Rose was well aware that of the two of them Sally had the better brain, but she resented almost as much as her sister the sort of attitude, still quite common among men of their acquaintance, that said plainly enough that they ought not to bother their pretty heads about such things. Sally would like the way Frank treated a woman as an equal, Rose was sure of that. And Sally would also be well-disposed to him because he had had a hard childhood, for Sally was always on the side of the underdog. It was a pity, thought Rose, that Sally had been so worn out that she had not been able to be properly introduced to Frank, but that was understandable enough after the long journey, and it was an omission that would soon be remedied. In short, this first very brief encounter between the two beings who were to share her heart between them had given Rose Livingstone no reason to fear that they would not soon draw close to each other.

While the one sister was thus drifting contentedly into sleep, the other lay in a state of agitated exhaustion of both mind and body that was almost beyond bearing. In whatever position she lay she could still feel the movement of the ship, and hear the throb of its engines. But in fact the most tolerable moments for Sally in this sleepless night were those when she had temporarily lost the sense of where she was and believed herself back on the SS *Rutlandshire*, a darkened ship steaming in darkness through dangerous seas. Then she would jerk into full consciousness again and know herself to be lying in Rose's bed in their London home. And with the image of Rose came also the image of the face that was so vivid in her memory, and the horror of the memory held her rigid in the bed. These phases of paralysis were succeeded by fits of doubt, during which it seemed quite impossible that the man Rose had engaged herself to marry could have the same face as the man Sally had seen pushing a woman's body through a porthole into dark waters.

It was impossible that Rose should fall in love with a murderer. Therefore there must be some other explanation. Either the man had a double, or else Sally as a child had imagined it all. But Christian Hofmeyr had taken her story seriously and had said she was not the sort of person to have hallucinations; and Uncle James, who was a good judge of character when one discounted his own peculiar view of the world, greatly disliked Frank, while Sally's mother, who was very easily taken in, liked him very much. As for Rose herself, there was no doubt in Sally's mind about her complete ignorance and complete sincerity. Sally knew only too well Rose's fears and weaknesses, and she had often worried lest Rose should be attracted towards just such a man as Frank Sedgemore seemed to be.

But never in her most extreme flights of anxiety had it occurred to her that Rose could love a murderer.

Once having allowed this thought to frame itself in her mind, Sally found it impossible to get rid of it. This marriage has to be stopped, she said to herself, even if I have to tell Rose the truth, even if I have to confront Frank with the truth.

After coming to this decision Sally gained a little rest at last, but at about eight o'clock in the morning, when everybody else in the flat was still sound asleep, she dressed quickly and let herself quietly out of the front door. All she had intended to do was telephone Chris from the call-box over the road, but when she saw a number 74 bus drawing up at the stop outside Park Mansions she jumped on to it without stopping to think, and was carried round to the other side of the park. She got off there and walked a little way, trying to picture Chris in her mind, and finding it very difficult to do so. She could feel him as a comforting and reassuring presence, and also, paradoxically, as a disturbing and rather mysterious presence, but she found it impossible to call up a clear image of his face. But what does that matter, she told herself impatiently; he is expecting me to ring him, he told me not to leave it too long before telling him; I was going to tell him in any case, and now I've something to add to the story, that's all.

She found a public telephone box and took from her purse two pennies and the slip of paper on which she had written Christian's telephone number. Once again she had the curious sensation of being at a critical moment in her life, pulled in two different ways by two equally strong forces. Don't phone him, said one voice; you've said too much already; leave ill alone and forget the whole thing. If Chris gets in touch with you, then tell him you've thought the whole thing over and are quite sure now that you imagined the incident on the boat. But I must tell somebody, cried the other voice; I can't go through with it alone. I can't keep up a pretence with Rose and Frank; I'll put my foot in it, I might even put Rose into danger . . . I have simply got to have some help and advice. Then why don't you talk to Uncle James, said the first voice, at the very moment that Sally was dialling Christian's number.

It was the first time this idea had come into her head, and it had a lot to recommend it. Even the part of Sally that was so much longing to see Chris again realized that. Of course Uncle James was the right person to tell. Much better than Charles Brent or any other of her friends. Uncle James was as safe as the Bank of England, and he already disliked Frank Sedgemore, so he would be willing to listen to what Sally said. But for that very reason perhaps she should not tell him, popped up the other voice when the ringing sound came on. Suppose she was completely mistaken and Frank Sedgemore had nothing to do with the man on the boat. Wouldn't she be accusing an innocent man and ruining Rose's happiness by putting Uncle James on his track?

Sally was rescued from the pendulum swing by the sound of the voice at the other end of the line giving the number, a low pleasant voice with a South African accent that sounded more marked on the telephone than it had done face to face.

'Is that Dr Hofmeyr?' asked Sally.

'Speaking.'

'Oh, Chris. It's me. Sally. I'm awfully sorry to disturb you so early. But something's happened – something connected with what we were talking about – and I urgently need your advice.'

'Where are you phoning from?'

'Near Gloucester Gate.'

'Then you're only five minutes from me. You'd better come round straight away.'

'But is that all right? I mean, I didn't wake you, did I? Are you up?'

'I'm up and dressed and in my right mind and actually having breakfast.' His voice sounded rather amused, and Sally began to relax. 'Come and join me,' he added.

'For breakfast?' she said doubtfully.

'Why not?' Chris laughed. 'Do you think it sounds too frightfully dissipated to be invited out for breakfast? I assure you it will be very meagre. Tea and crispbread and marmalade.'

'I'll look forward to it,' said Sally. 'Won't be long.'

She put down the receiver feeling considerably better. He had sounded just the same as when they had first begun to talk and laugh together on board the SS *Rutlandshire*, and it was difficult now to understand why she had had any doubts about getting in touch with him.

The flat was reassuring, too. As Sally arrived on the doorstep of the modest terrace house, a plump, cheerful-looking woman in a dressing-gown opened the door and stooped to pick up two bottles of milk.

'Which bell is Dr Hofmeyr's?' asked Sally.

'Middle one,' replied the woman. 'Is he expecting you?'

'Yes.'

'Then there's no need to ring. Come on in.'

She held open the front door, and continued to talk as they climbed the stairs. 'I was so glad to see him back. Not that I'm nervous, exactly, but my husband's been put on night shift – he's in munitions – and it's nice to feel there'll be someone else in the place at night if we get a raid.'

'It is indeed,' replied Sally. There was something very normal and comforting about the woman with her peroxide hair and slight Cockney accent, and about the stairs with the brown and green linoleum and the smell of polish. There were two doors, both painted brown, on the first-floor landing, and in response to a knock at one of them Chris appeared and greeted Sally and thanked her companion.

'You'll be wanting some more milk, doctor,' said the plump woman. 'Here's a pint and you can pay me back when you get yourself straight.'

'That's awfully good of you, Mrs Martin,' said Christian. 'I'll get my housekeeping going today and stop sponging on you.'

'You're welcome,' said Mrs Martin. 'Bye for now.' She gave Sally a quick appraising glance, and then hurried on upstairs to the top flat.

'I hope I haven't ruined your reputation with your neighbours,' said Sally, as she followed Christian into a fair-sized room with two sash windows overlooking the street. It was, as he had said, adequately furnished. There were two bulging bookcases, and she noticed that he had

45

been reading some letters that lay on the table between the windows. On the walls were some Van Gogh reproductions, but no photographs, nor any other evidence of his own personal tastes. But he admits to being rather a rolling stone, she said to herself, and in any case, some people don't leave their mark on their surroundings.

'You've probably made Mrs Martin's day,' said Chris in reply to Sally's remark. 'Ever since I came here she's been dying for me to have some lady visitors.'

'How long have you had the flat?'

'About a year.'

'And I'm the first female to have crossed the threshold since then?'

Christian laughed. 'Wouldn't you like to know? Come and have some tea. You'd better make the best of it while you can. It'll be rationed before long.'

'Tea! Rationed!' cried Sally. 'Heavens! What on earth shall we do? England will most certainly lose the war.'

Christian laughed again. 'I dare say we'll survive. We'll just have to, won't we? Anything that can't be grown in this island will only come here at great risk to lives and to shipping.'

'And tea doesn't grow in England,' said Sally more soberly. 'You know, Chris, when I really start thinking about the war I feel ashamed to be so taken up with my own personal affairs.'

'We dealt with that one yesterday on the boat,' he replied. 'Here you are, seeking my advice, and here am I, willing to help you if I can.'

'All right then, here goes. I only hope you're going to believe me.'

46

Sally raised her eyes from her plate and looked at him doubtfully. The long face was now as sombre as her own. The eyes behind the big glasses surveyed her with an unfathomable expression.

'Well, what has happened, Sally?' he asked in his quietest and most restrained manner.

'I've seen that face again,' she said, watching him for signs of disbelief and seeing none. In fact, he gave a quite noticeable start.

'Good God,' he cried, and then added with a smile that seemed to come with something of an effort this time: 'This isn't just an elaborate joke, is it, Sally?'

'It's no joke at all,' she replied with a hint of sharpness. 'I know I've got a peculiar sense of humour but I'm not making this one up. I'm worried to death.'

'I'm sorry,' He put out a hand across the table to still her restless fingers as they pulled at the edge of the cloth. 'It gave me rather a shock, hearing you say that. I didn't expect quite such a quick reaction to our conversation yesterday.'

'Reaction?' Sally pulled her hand away and gripped her fingers together. 'Reaction? Do you mean you think my telling you about that man on the boat has started my mind working in such a way that I'm imagining I've seen him?'

'You have got a brain, haven't you?' he said, and even in the agitation of the moment Sally could not help but feel flattered by the genuine admiration in his voice. To be admired for her ability and character rather than for her looks was something she had always craved and seldom experienced.

'Well, that's what it sounded like,' she retorted in a

brisk but somewhat mollified voice. 'You're the one who knows about the workings of the mind, not me. But even I can see that telling you about that memory of mine yesterday could stir things up in me so much that I might actually project – project is the word, isn't it? – actually project my thoughts on to somebody outside. Isn't that what you think has happened, Chris?'

'My dear girl, you have taken the words out of my mouth. You have also taken me down a peg and made me feel very humble.' Christian smiled again, and this time it was the genuine thing. 'You're very good for me, Sally,' he went on. 'I'm inclined to think too much of myself. But to return to the business in hand, you must admit that it was a bit surprising. I left you last night in the bosom of your family, and first thing this morning you tell me you've seen your unknown murderer. If he was a murderer and if you really did see him. It's quick work, isn't it?'

Sally began to laugh. 'Put like that it does sound a bit dotty,' she admitted. 'I should have told you straight away. It's Rose's fiancé. They came in together late last night, and I just caught a glimpse of him and recognized the face at once.'

'Your sister's fiancé,' repeated Christian. 'How very extraordinary.'

He sounded intrigued rather than shocked, and Sally felt comforted, feeling sure now that he did not disbelieve her.

'It's not only extraordinary,' she said, 'it's also very worrying. I've been lying awake all night wondering what to do. Ought I to warn Rose? Ought I to try to stop the marriage? That's what I want your advice about.'

'If you were absolutely certain' said Christian slowly, 'that you knew something to the detriment of the man your sister proposed to marry, then clearly you ought seriously to consider taking some drastic action. But you aren't absolutely certain, are you, Sally?'

'When I saw him I was sure it was the same face,' she said stubbornly.

'How are you going to prove it? Assuming this incident on the boat really happened, how do you propose to prove that the man you saw last night is the same person as the man on the boat?'

'I don't know how I'm going to prove it. I was hoping you might help me.' He did not immediately respond, and she added, a little reproachfully: 'You did offer to help me sort out my memories and get over my phobia, didn't you?'

'I did indeed, but I was thinking in terms of psychotherapy, not of detective work involving another person. However.' He seemed to come to a decision. 'The main thing is to set your mind at rest, so let's start right in on it now. First of all, you'd better tell me the full story of the incident on the boat, but since this is obviously going to take some time I'll go and make some fresh tea.'

'And I'd better phone home,' said Sally, 'if you don't mind. They'll be wondering where I am. I'll tell them I've come to see an old school friend of mine who lives not far from here. And by the way, Chris.'

He paused with the tray in his hands at the door leading into the kitchen, and said: 'Yes, ma'am?'

'If tea's going to be rationed, d'you think we could have

the next pot a bit stronger? Indulge ourselves today, for tomorrow we die.'

'These South Africans,' retorted Christian. 'They're even worse tannin-addicts than the English, and that's saying a lot.'

Chapter Five

THIS LIGHTENED MOOD lasted for a little longer.

'I got through to Mother,' said Sally when Christian returned with a replenished tray, 'and she said, "Oh well, if they don't mind you eating their food, I'm sure I don't mind." Then I spoke to Uncle James, and he said if I was walking back through the park would I take care, because he thinks they've got an anti-aircraft gun emplacement there somewhere, and personally he wouldn't trust the gunners with a child's popgun, since none of them have been properly trained. Then I got Mother again and she said did I realize I wasn't to go anywhere without a gas mask and identity card, and then Uncle James grabbed the phone back and said it was a lot of damn tomfoolery, all this gas-mask business, and then Rose came along and said don't be long because she was dying to talk to me properly and didn't I think the silver barrage balloons looked pretty against the blue sky.'

Christian laughed heartily. 'I had much the same conversation with my good neighbour Mrs Martin last night,' he said. 'This gas-mask business seems to have become an obsession. I suppose it's something tangible to hold on to and gives people a feeling of security.'

'Go on,' said Sally when he paused for a moment. 'I'd

love to hear your lecture on the psychology of civilians in war-time. It sounds fascinating.'

'I certainly find it interesting,' he said sobering up, 'but it had better wait until another time. We've got more urgent business on hand.'

He looked at her expectantly, and Sally suddenly found herself extremely reluctant to talk about her own dilemma. Indeed, for the last few minutes she had managed to put it right out of her mind, and had been enjoying Christian's company as much as she had enjoyed it on the voyage. If only I had never told him about that business at all, she said to herself, then we could have grown to be real friends on equal terms and I'd have learnt more about him, and later on perhaps I could have told him. If only their positions could now be reversed, with Chris the one who was about to reveal something in his own past, and Sally ready to listen and advise. But there was no going back now, and there was also no doubt that she did badly need a confidant.

'Where shall I begin?' she asked.

'Wherever you like. Tell it your own way. I'm going to sit more comfortably.'

He got up from the table and gestured to Sally to take one of the big leather armchairs while he took the other. This meant that they were no longer sitting opposite to each other but were both facing the gas-fire. It was a battered old fire, with the asbestos candles cracked and even broken in places, and the blue flame flickered unevenly. Surrounding it were green tiles and above them was a wooden mantelpiece stained dark brown, on which stood a heavy square glass ashtray and an angular green and orange vase. Sally was not normally a particularly observant girl, being more interested in people than in places, but these objects imprinted themselves on her eyes as her mind withdrew into the past, so that it seemed as if her own internal drama was being played out against a backdrop of a broken gas fire and its immediate surroundings.

'We were on the *Cape St Vincent*,' she said. 'We'd just left Tenerife. The Cape and County boats used to stop there for a day. But of course you know that.' She shifted slightly in her chair, but did not turn to look at Christian. 'They picked up bananas and tomatoes. We anchored out in the harbour and there were little boats coming and going all the time collecting and delivering things, and people went ashore, and others came aboard and set up a sort of market in the well-deck, and little native boys came and dived over the side of the ship. The sea was perfectly calm and blue. I can see it now. It's like a vivid dream.'

Sally leant back in her chair and shut her eyes. The blue sea and the dark rugged outline of the island superimposed themselves on the broken gas-fire in her mental vision.

'I wasn't so ill that day,' she continued, opening her eyes again and staring straight ahead. 'It was having the ship not moving, I suppose. And the sight of land, and feeling I could actually go and stand on some land. Of course, I wasn't fit to go ashore, but I was able to come up to the promenade deck and take notice of what was going on. I sat in a deckchair out of the sun, and Rose wanted to stay with me, but Mother dragged her off to go and buy things. It was two days before Christmas, and people were getting presents for each other, and there was to be a fancy-dress party on Christmas Eve.'

Again Sally shifted in her chair, and this time she did

glance at Christian, because she had had the impression that he had made some sound or reacted in some way to her last words. But his face was perfectly calm and unmoved as he too looked at the gas-fire and murmured, 'Christmas on board. Yes, I once spent Christmas on board.'

Sally resumed her unseeing staring and her story.

'The deck steward brought me some lemonade and an egg sandwich. It was the first food I'd been able to have for days, and it tasted wonderful. He was quite an elderly man, and he stayed and talked to me, and I told him how much I missed my Dad, and he told me about his folks in England. He also gave me some advice about how to cope with seasickness and said I'd probably be better when I was older, which I was, but that I'd never entirely get rid of it, which I haven't.'

Sally smiled faintly, re-living a pleasant memory.

'He was such a nice old chap,' she went on. 'I never saw him again, because that was the last time I was able to sit up on deck. We talked a long time, and I remember asking him about all the comings and goings of people from the boat to the island, and didn't anybody ever get left behind or taken on to England by mistake, and he said they had sometimes had a stowaway. I found that very exciting, like a boys' school story. I used to love boys' school stories. Talbot Baines Reed.'

Again Sally paused for a moment, smiling to herself, before continuing. 'The deck steward said he'd try to find me a book I'd enjoy, but I don't think he ever did. I don't remember any more of that day. I must have started to be sick again when the ship moved, and the next thing I remember clearly is all the fuss about whether I would be well enough to go to the Christmas Eve fancy dress party. Rose was as bad as Mother about it. I've only been really angry with Rose two or three times in my life, and this was one of them. Or rather, I would have been angry if I hadn't been so feeble. Why is it, Chris—' and Sally turned to face the man sitting silently in the other big arm-chair—'that people can't understand that when you are very seasick all you want is for them to leave you alone and let you die?'

'As a non-sufferer myself,' he replied, 'I should guess it is because they feel so helpless. With most complaints nowadays we can at least do something to bring temporary relief, if not permanent improvement, but we have not yet discovered a drug that will control nausea. It's very frustrating to feel that you can't help at all, and I suppose this can make you feel a little impatient with the sufferer. But don't despair. Research is always going on. One day we'll find a way to ease it.'

'Let's hope so,' said Sally, resuming her former posture and her own journey into the past. 'It really was utter misery. We had a four-berth cabin, but it was very small. Like a railway sleeping compartment. I was in one of the lower bunks so that I could get out quickly and go to the bathroom, which was next to us, luckily. If I didn't make it in time and hadn't got a bowl handy then I was sick into the washbasin which was between the two sets of bunks. Sometimes I didn't even get that far. It can't have been much fun having to share a tiny cabin with me, but of course I didn't think of that at the time, only about how miserable I was. And of course I didn't want to miss the party – I always loved parties – but it was obvious that I couldn't possibly go, and I was just longing for them to go

55

and leave me in peace and stop arguing about who was to sit with me. I didn't want either of them. It was bad enough having to hear about all their preparations, with Mother dressing up as Boadicea and Rose as a shepherdess. And the whole ship seemed to be buzzing with it. I could feel all the excitement, even just lying there in the cabin.

'It's extraordinary,' went on Sally, staring at the gasfire but not seeing it, 'how some memories are perfectly clear and others are gone completely. What makes us remember some things and not others? Anyway,' she continued hastily, suddenly remembering that she was talking to a man whose special interest was the functioning of the human mind, and not wanting her story to be interrupted by a lecture on psychology just at this stage, 'what happened next is perfectly clear. After Mother and Rose had gone the stewardess came along with yet more beef tea and started fussing over me. I told her I only wanted to go to sleep, and she said I was to ring the bell if I needed anything or felt lonely and she would come at once. I don't think there was anybody in any of the cabins near us. After she'd gone I think I really did go to sleep for a while, and when I woke up I actually felt a bit better, and I thought that even if I had to miss all the real fun, at least I could have some sort of little adventure of my own that nobody else would know about. So I decided to explore our little corner of the ship, knowing there wouldn't be anybody about. It sounds a bit silly, but then kids do like to explore – girls as well as boys – even when they're seasick. I thought I'd start with the bathroom next door. I'd been in there plenty of times, of course, but never had a chance to look around, and it rather fascinated me. It must have been built right into the curve of the ship at the bows, with part of the floor sloping – like an attic upside down – and on the sloping side there was a wide ledge a little way up from the floor. It was like a window-seat, except that there wasn't a window, only the porthole above the ledge. It had been open a lot of the time when we were in the tropics, and I'd always wanted to climb up on the ledge and look out of the porthole to see how far down the water was, but I'd always either had somebody with me or been feeling too ill. So that was my first aim, although I thought I'd probably have to get the porthole open myself, since it was very stormy and they would surely have shut it.

'Actually, the ship was rolling terribly. Mother's dressing-gown hung on a hook on the back of the cabin door, and I could see it swaying like a pendulum. When I got out of my bunk I had to cling hard to its side, and then to the door of the cabin, which came open right at me when I got near it. I got outside the cabin and hung on to the rail that ran along the corridor, and I remember feeling very giddy but sort of excited at the same time. It was a challenge I'd set myself – to have a look through the porthole, even if I couldn't explore any further. I was determined to do it, and I knew I'd feel much happier if I managed to. The bathroom door was shut, which rather surprised me, because usually it was wedged open when it wasn't in use, and I didn't see how it could be in use with everyone gone to the party. I hadn't heard anybody come along our corridor, but of course I'd been asleep, and besides there was always such a lot of creaking and groaning of the ship that you didn't always hear people coming unless they were talking loudly. But I do remember wondering whether to go back to the cabin and come out again later, because I didn't want anybody to come out of the bathroom and find me.

'However, the problem was solved by the ship giving a terrific roll, and the bathroom door swinging open with a crash just as the cabin door had done. The locks and bolts can't have been very efficient. So I saw it all, suddenly, in a flash like lightning.'

Sally gave a little involuntary shudder and instinctively put up her hands to cover her eyes as if she had indeed been struck by some violent natural phenomenon.

'The bathroom light must have been on,' she said presently, letting her hands fall to the arms of the chair once more. 'I'm sure it was after dark, but I certainly saw clearly. He was standing up on the ledge near the porthole, bending over so that his head didn't touch the ceiling, and he'd got his arms round something that was half in and half out of the porthole. Of course, I only saw the half that was in the bathroom. There was a bit of red skirt, and there were legs in light-coloured stockings and high-heeled black patent leather shoes. He'd been looking towards the porthole, I think, and turned his head to look towards the door when it flew open, and I was standing in the open doorway, hanging on to the rail at the side, so we were face to face, only a few yards apart. I saw his face as clearly as I can see yours now.'

Sally turned to face Christian. 'And he must have seen mine as clearly as you can see me.'

There was a moment's silence while they gazed at each other, both with very serious expressions and then Sally cried in quite a different tone of voice: 'Good God! What's that?'

58

'Air-raid warning,' said Christian, speaking loudly to try to beat the noise. They looked at each other in some consternation while the siren continued its loud wail, lurching between its two notes for what seemed a very long time.

At last came the relief of silence, but it was not a peaceful silence. It was tense with apprehension.

'Do you think it's really starting?' whispered Sally, trying hard to adjust herself to the sudden jump from the shocks of the past to the shocks of the present.

'It could be a genuine raid, I suppose,' replied Christian, 'but it's more likely a false alarm. Mrs Martin says this happens now and then. Either that or the civil defence people get bored and set off the sirens for fun.'

'I don't think there's much fun about it,' said Sally. 'I feel as if it's split my eardrums. What a ghastly noise.'

'Bombs will be even louder.'

'Ought we to take cover or something?'

'There's some sort of shelter in the park, I believe. Or we could go and sit on the floor in the front hall. Does it really worry you, Sally?'

'No, not really,' she replied. 'I'm feeling a bit jittery, but it's because of what I've been talking about, not the siren at all. It was a terrible shock, you know, when I suddenly saw that man pushing a woman through the porthole, and I think I must have been reliving it.'

'You have most certainly been reliving it,' said Christian. 'I've been watching you while you were talking, and I could see you were. But you'd nearly finished, so if you could manage to . . . There you are.' He interrupted himself. 'That's the all-clear. False alarm.'

They waited until the sound of the high-pitched single note had died away.

'Where was I?' asked Sally.

'You were standing in the open doorway of a bathroom on one of the lower decks of a Cape and County vessel that had just called at Tenerife and in front of you was a man standing on a ledge with his arms round what looked like half the body of a woman. It sounds rather like a conjuring trick,' added Christian lightly. 'The sawing-a-lady-in-half act.'

'Maybe that's what he'd done,' said Sally in a similar tone of voice. 'I certainly didn't see the other half.'

'No doubt it was already fed to the sharks. I'm sorry,' he added in a different manner. 'I hope you don't think I'm not taking you seriously just because I sound rather flippant. I assure you I am taking you very seriously indeed. Just how much so you will see in a moment. But first you had better finish. What happened next?'

'Nothing actually happened. We stared at each other, and then the ship heaved right over to the other side, and the bathroom door came crashing shut and stayed shut this time.'

'And what did little Sally Livingstone do?'

'Little Sally Livingstone decided that she had had quite enough exploring. She got back to the cabin somehow, and shut the door behind her, and shot the bolt, and made quite sure that it was really fixed. After that she was very sick in the washbasin, and that held her attention for quite a while, during which she was not aware that anybody rattled the door or tried to get into the cabin or passed along the corridor or anything else. When her insides had calmed down a little she lay on the bunk in a state of collapse and eventually she managed to ring the bell. She was a bit nervous about opening the door, and only did so when she heard the stewardess's voice. The stewardess suggested beef tea again, but all that little Sally Livingstone wanted was to know whether the stewardess had heard or seen anything. The stewardess asked what I meant, and I said I had seen a man in the bathroom. She must have gone to look because I remember her coming into the cabin and saying that there was nobody there and I must have dreamed it. I expect I was in quite a state by this time, what with being both sick and terrified, and I believe I said something about being frightened of drowning and that must have convinced her that I was either hysterical or delirious or both. She took my temperature and sent for the doctor, and when he came along I started raving to him. I suppose it sounded like raving. The doctor asked me what the man looked like, and I said he'd got a long white coat, and the doctor said, "I've got on a white coat. Was it me that you saw?"'

Sally paused for breath. Christian got up and went into the other room. He came back wearing a white hospital coat over his brown suit and said to Sally: 'I've got on a doctor's white coat. Was it me that you saw?'

Sally looked up at him in astonishment.

'Of course not. No more than it was the ship's doctor. What on earth is the matter with you, Chris? Is this meant to be a joke?'

'Not entirely. I have a serious purpose, as I said. I should like to demonstrate to you the problems of identification.'

'But I know about the problems of identification. Have you forgotten our favourite detective-story writers? I

61

know all about identity parades and different witnesses picking out different people, even when it was somebody they had seen only last week.'

'Exactly,' said Christian. 'Only last week. Sometimes only yesterday, and often for much longer than just a moment. Do you remember that little man in the blue beret who walked round and round the deck on the *Rutlandshire*?'

'Of course I remember him,' said Sally.

'Suppose ten men of somewhat similar appearance were to stand in front of you at this moment. Would you be able to pick out our little man?'

'I don't know,' admitted Sally. 'I wouldn't like to swear to it. But this was different.'

'Why was it different?' asked Christian, and then continued more gently before Sally had a chance to reply: 'I hope you don't think I'm cross-examining you just for the fun of it, Sally. I'm simply trying to help you get things in proportion so that we can weigh up the odds in favour of your recognizing this man before you actually do anything drastic.'

'I quite understand that,' said Sally with spirit, 'and I'm glad to be attacked because it makes me think harder, get it all into proportion, as you say. But I still say that you can't compare my problem to that of picking out a little man in a blue beret.'

'Why not?'

'Because I don't care a damn about the little man in the blue beret!' cried Sally banging her fist on the arm of the chair. 'He didn't do anything to make me notice him. He was just one of the people on board. I'd already have forgotten him if you hadn't reminded me. I shall most certainly have forgotten him ten years from now. But a man pushing a woman into the sea – that's not the sort of thing you see every day, nor even every year. That's the sort of thing you aren't likely to forget.'

'You've made your point,' said Christian. 'I have to admit there's a difference. On the other hand, when the police hold an identification parade it sometimes is because the witness has seen somebody commit an offence. It does not necessarily follow that the witness is able to recognize the offender beyond all question of doubt.'

'If they'd seen him as clearly as I did,' said Sally, 'and if the man was as easily distinguishable—'

'How was he distinguishable? What did he actually look like?'

'He was tall and thin—'

'About my height? About my build?'

'Yes, I should say so,' said Sally, looking at Christian who was standing in front of her chair, still wearing the white hospital coat.

'What shaped face?' he asked.

'Rather long and—'

'Long and narrow like mine?' broke in Christian.

'Yes,' said Sally. 'I think it was.'

'And what colouring? What sort of hair and eyes?'

'Dark skin, dark hair, dark eyes, all not unlike yours!' cried Sally speaking in a rush before Christian could interrupt again. 'I've got your point, and I'm not denying that there are plenty of tall, thin men with longish faces and dark colouring in the world in addition to the man on the boat. I can think of—' and she paused for a moment, frowning—'at least three I know well who answer that description. That's not counting you or Frank Sedge-more. It's never occurred to me to suspect any of those three of being the man I saw. Then none of them have any scars on their face. But Frank's got a half-circle scar on the left cheek, just like the man I saw on the *Cape St Vincent*.'

Christian took off the white coat and laid it over the back of a chair and then sat down again. 'A scar is certainly a distinguishing mark,' he said in his most impersonal manner, 'but even that can be faked. People who do the make-up for film actors are very good at it.'

'Why on earth should Frank Sedgemore go around with a faked scar?'

'I've no idea why your sister's fiancé should do so, but I can make a few guesses. It was fancy dress party night. Perhaps the scar was part of the fancy dress. And the white coat, too.'

'Oh.' For the first time there was some hesitation in Sally's voice. 'I never thought of that. But what sort of fancy dress could it be?'

'Some sort of character from fiction perhaps. I'm not very good at this sort of inventiveness. But quite apart from that, has it ever occurred to you that you may have misinterpreted what you saw? That the man may have been trying to pull the woman back through the porthole, not pushing her out? That he may in fact have been rescuing a would-be suicide?'

Sally thought this over for a minute or two. Christian's barrage of questions, that had at first had the effect of strengthening her own conviction, was now making her more and more doubtful and bewildered. She did not mind him testing her memory in this way, because it seemed to her a sensible way to proceed, but it was not quite what she had expected when he had said he would help her to sort out her memories. What she did rather resent, however, was the sense of being subtly manipulated, of being forced more and more into a position where she felt less and less able to say, 'I know this for a certainty.' Of course, there was a reason for this: if she told her story to anybody else, if she challenged Frank himself with it, she would certainly have to stand up to this sort of questioning, but she could not help suspecting that Christian was aiming to increase her self-doubt rather than to reinforce her belief. Why he should want to do this she did not dare let herself consider. She had the feeling of having embarked on a journey as full of hidden dangers as the voyage of the *Rutlandshire* had been; a feeling that her own life was at the mercy of torpedoes against which she had no defence, and it was too late to turn back.

'I suppose it could just be that he was pulling her in and not pushing her out,' she said at last, 'but I don't think so. I've a feeling there was something about the position of his arms . . . I certainly had the strong impression that he was in process of pushing her out. In any case, if someone had tried to commit suicide that way, surely it would have been talked about on the boat.'

'Surely not in front of the children!'

'You don't know my mother. She loves scandal, and has never minded how much we heard. Talking of Mother,' continued Sally, getting to her feet, 'I really must be going now. I'll have to see about that gas-mask and all the rest of the paraphernalia. And you ought to be getting on with your own affairs.'

'I most certainly ought.' He accompanied her down the stairs. 'I feel I've let you down, Sally,' he said at the front door. 'I promised to try to help with your water phobia, and we haven't even mentioned it.'

'But we've certainly sorted out my memories,' she said.

'I'm glad you think so. After saying I was going to concentrate on the psychological rather than the detective aspect, I seem to have been doing just the opposite, and setting up your story as a target for the defence lawyer or the private investigator to break down.'

'That's certainly what it felt like,' she replied, 'but it's been very useful to me. I feel I know much more where to go from here.'

'You won't do anything hasty, I hope?'

'Tell Frank Sedgemore that I think he's a murderer? No, Chris, I won't do that. You've talked me out of that one, and I'm most grateful. I feel I can face him now and put on a suitable act. Maybe when I next meet him I won't even see his face as the same as the man on the boat. Maybe it's just as you suspected – that the stirring up of memories caused me to see it that way.'

'Personally I think that's the most likely explanation,' said Christian, 'but whether you will be able to accept it is another matter. Knowing you, I fear you will not be content to let it rest there.'

'Knowing me, I fear I won't. But I'll go carefully. Thanks again, Chris. You've helped a lot.'

Sally held out her hand, and he held it for a moment. 'Let's meet again,' he said, 'and talk about other things. I presume some of the London restaurants are still functioning. How about a decent dinner instead of a skimpy breakfast?'

'That would be lovely.'

'May I telephone you at home? Or would you still rather I didn't?'

'Ring me at home,' replied Sally. 'I can't think why I was so silly about it yesterday. It's not as if you were some dark and mysterious villain out of a spy thriller, is it? You're a perfectly respectable South African doctor whom I got friendly with on the boat.'

'I am a perfectly respectable South African doctor with whom you made friends on the boat,' repeated Christian gravely, 'and I won't let you down in front of the family.'

Chapter Six

SALLY GOT BACK to Park Mansions to find a battle going on between her mother and uncle on the one side, and her sister on the other. She need not have feared any questions about her early morning outing, because none of them showed any interest in what she had been doing; all were too intent on claiming her as an ally.

'Perhaps you'll be able to talk some sense into Rose,' said Mrs Livingstone to Sally. 'She can't possibly stay here in London by herself. Or even the two of you together,' she added, belatedly remembering that she now had both her daughters in England.

'Much better come back to Oxford with me,' said Uncle James. 'You too, Sal. Plenty of room for the lot of you at Weir House. Please Gertrude, too. Always been fond of you girls.'

'Oh Sally, I'm so glad you're back!' cried Rose, hugging her sister, and making Sally feel guilty for having spent so much time with Chris. 'Mother and Uncle James want us all to move to Oxford because they think we'll be safer there, but I'm not in the least frightened of air-raids, and I'd much rather stay in London and be with Frank. And with you,' she added quickly, but not quickly enough to escape Sally's notice. 'Why can't Sally and I stay here together,' she went on, turning to her mother, 'while you go back with Uncle James? I'm sure Sally's not worried about air-raids either.'

'You may not be worried, but I should never have a moment's peace for worry about you,' said Mrs Livingstone, 'and I think it's very selfish of you, Rose, to put yourself into danger like that.'

'Mind you,' said Uncle James in a placatory tone of voice, 'we don't know yet that there's all that danger. And for all we know they may bomb Oxford.'

'James!' Sarah Livingstone turned an outraged face on her brother. 'How can you let me down like this? Why have they evacuated the children, and why is everyone leaving London, if there's no special danger?'

Uncle James muttered something about panic measures, never did approve of them.

'And anyway,' continued Sarah Livingstone, 'it's perfectly absurd to say they may bomb Oxford. Everybody knows that Oxford is the last place that would be bombed.'

'Why won't they bomb Oxford?' asked Sally, really interested for once in hearing what her mother had to say.

'Because Hitler has friends there whom he wouldn't want to suffer.'

'Hitler's friends! What on earth do you mean, Mother?' cried Sally. 'If there's a nest of Nazi spies in Oxford I most certainly wouldn't want to be living there myself. Anyway, oughtn't the powers-that-be to know about it?'

'There's no spies in Oxford,' said Uncle James giving his sister a warning glance. 'Just a silly rumour. Better not say any more. Never does any good to gossip. It's against the law now, anyway.'

'What d'you feel, Sally?' said Rose, who had been

waiting impatiently to get a word in. 'Shall we stay here? Or do air-raids really worry you?'

'They don't worry me at the moment,' said Sally, 'but that may only be because I've never been in one.'

She knew that this was not quite what Rose had wanted her to say, but for all her love for her sister Sally could not view with whole-hearted enthusiasm the prospect of remaining in London to make a threesome with Rose and Frank. If she had liked and trusted Frank it would have been different, but even if she could convince herself that he was not the man on the boat, Sally felt that she would still dislike him. Having others present would take off some of the awkwardness, but if the three of them were to be much together she did not know how she would be able to hide her own feelings. On the other hand, the proposed arrangement would give her a good opportunity to carry out the task she had set herself, which was to investigate thoroughly the past life and present activities of Frank Sedgemore, not to mention the fact that if she were to leave London she would be unlikely to see Chris again.

Sally had to admit to herself that this last was the deciding factor. The long talk that she had had with Chris that morning had only increased his fascination for her, and the fact that there was now something rather frightening about the mystery that seemed to surround him only added to the appeal. Sally was as determined to fathom this mystery as she was to investigate Frank. Why had Chris put himself forward so strongly as a possible candidate for the man on the boat? There were plenty of other ways of convincing her of the difficulties of identification, and yet he had to choose that one. It was almost as if he wanted her to suspect that he could himself be the man, but why he should want that Sally could not begin to guess; she only knew that she would never rest until she had found the answer.

'I think I should like to stay in London,' she said in reply to a question from Uncle James. 'It's not that I'm not grateful to you and Auntie Gertrude, but I really do want to do something in the war effort, and that will be easier in London.'

'That settles it, then,' cried Rose hugging her sister again. 'We'll be all right, Uncle James,' she added, embracing her uncle in turn. 'You don't need to worry about me now Sally's here.'

'If Sally hadn't come back,' said Mrs Livingstone bitterly, 'there'd be no question of Rose not coming to Oxford.'

'Mother!' crid Rose. 'How can you? It's absolutely wonderful having Sally home.'

James Davenant made a similar protest, but nothing that her uncle and sister could say could save Sally's feelings. She believed that she knew her mother through and through. She believed that she had written off her mother completely as far as affection or loyalty or any good feeling of any kind was concerned, and yet for all her reasoning and her resignation she was still capable of being terribly hurt. And, being Sally, she was not able to be hurt without hitting back.

'If that's how you feel,' she said, 'then it really is a pity I didn't stay in Cape Town.'

Rose and Uncle James hurried in to smooth things over, and their combined efforts produced an uneasy truce for a short while.

'I suppose you'll have to stay here,' said Sarah Living-

71

stone very grudgingly, 'but I still think it's extremely selfish. Even if you don't care about my feelings, you might have had more consideration for your uncle's. You could at least have shown your gratitude for all he's done for you by saving him from the evacuees.'

'Saving him from the evacuees?' repeated Sally in bewilderment. 'Why is Uncle James in danger from the evacuees?'

'Oh really!' exclaimed Mrs Livingstone, and turned away to re-arrange a big vase of chrysanthemums, snapping off the ends of the stems and replacing the blooms with little sharp angry movements.

'Sally can't possibly know the position,' said Rose. 'She's only just arrived. They're sending all the children out of London and other big cities,' she explained to her sister, 'and billeting them on families in safer areas. It's the law now, one of the emergency regulations, and if they decide you've got adequate accommodation to take them you're not allowed to refuse.'

'Perfectly scandalous!' cried Mrs Livingstone with a particularly vicious little snap. 'As if there's not enough to put up with already without having your home invaded by filthy little brats from the East End of London! Their language is appalling, and they're covered with lice, and they don't even know how to use a lavatory. It's really too bad to ask decent people to put up with things like that. Really, I do think they ought to have more considera-tion.'

Both Rose and Uncle James began to speak, but their mild protests were drowned by an explosion from Sally.

'Decent people!' she shouted, taking a couple of strides towards her mother, and then suddenly stopping short

72

and holding her hands clenched by her sides. 'Decent people would be only too glad to help. Decent people would want to do their best for the poor little devils who haven't had a chance in life. It's not the fault of the kids if they are filthy and their language is appalling. It's the fault of our bloody rotten society that let them get like that and didn't care!'

'Don't you swear at me!' screamed Mrs Livingstone, advancing on her younger daughter with a bronze chrysanthemum held upright in her hand like a weapon. 'Don't you dare speak like that to me!'

'Our bloody rotten society!' yelled Sally back, 'and all the bloody snobs who think a posh house is more important than the welfare of our children!'

'Sally, Sally.' Rose was tugging at her arm, trying to calm her. 'I do agree with you, and so would Frank, but it's no good shouting at Mother.'

Sarah Livingstone screamed again, dropped the bronze chrysanthemum, and proceeded to go into hysterics. Rose let go of Sally's arm and rushed to her mother's side. James Davenant, who had been massaging the side of his face in an uneasy manner during this scene, came across the room to Sally and put an arm round her shoulders and said: 'Come on, Sal. Leave your mother alone. Rose is right. It's not her fault, and it's no good shouting at her. Matter of fact, I wouldn't at all mind taking in a couple of kids myself, poor little blighters. Feed 'em up and give 'em plenty of fresh air and teach them to hold a straight bat. It's your Aunt Gertrude who doesn't feel up to it, and you can't blame her. She's not as young as she was, and her heart's dicky, and we've very little help in the house now that everyone's off to do war work. Got to think of these things, y'know. It's never all that simple.'

'I'm sorry, Uncle James,' said Sally burying her face on his shoulder. 'I wasn't meaning anything against you or Auntie Gertrude. Truly I wasn't.'

'I know that, m'dear. Nor against your mother either, I hope.'

Sally raised her head, took a deep breath, and said in a flat voice: 'It's certainly not Mother's fault that there are so many uncared for children in this country. I'm sorry if I gave the impression that I thought it was.'

Mrs Livingstone, who had muted her hysterics in order to listen to this remark, gave a loud sniff, pushed Rose away, picked up the bronze chrysanthemum and began to re-arrange the flowers yet again. Behind her back James Davenant signalled to the two girls to leave the room with him.

'Got a suggestion to make,' he said when they were all three in the hall of the flat and the door of the big sitting-room was closed behind them. 'Put it to your mother when she's calmed down a bit. How about a compromise, eh? Good old British compromise. You two girls stay up here during the week and come down to Oxford at weekends. Gives you a chance to get a job in London, Sal, and saves your aunt from having to look after children, which she's not fitted for, not on any count. Well? How about it?'

'I think it's a good idea,' said Sally.

'I wonder if Mother will like it,' said Rose.

'You leave your mother to me. Do you like it, Rose? That's the thing.'

'Of course I do. But you won't mind, will you, Uncle

James, if I don't always come for the weekend, because sometimes Frank has a rush job on, and he likes me to help him.'

'H'm.' James Davenant glanced round and caught Sally's eye. 'H'm. Well in that case I suppose Sally had better stay here too.'

'You won't mind, darling, will you?' said Rose. 'I don't suppose it will happen very often.'

Sally found herself feeling very irritated with her sister, which was something quite new. It seemed to her that Rose had changed, and that it could only be Frank's doing. Her beloved Rose, nearest and dearest for all the twenty-two years that Sally had lived on the earth, had not only turned into a person who no longer put her sister first, which was understandable enough in the circumstances, but had also turned into a person who was somehow not quite straight and true. Sally did not know how she knew this, but she felt sure that Uncle James, who was still absolutely straight and true, knew it also, and that in that moment when they had caught each other's eye they had exchanged this knowledge.

'What sort of work is Frank doing,' Sally asked her sister, 'that might keep him busy over the weekend?'

'He runs this agency,' said Rose vaguely. 'A lot of people have been called up for military service and he has to attend to things himself.'

'What sort of things?' asked Sally bluntly.

'Clients,' said Rose even more vaguely. 'People who are busy during the week and haven't got time to attend to anything except at the weekends.'

'I still don't understand,' said Sally. 'Frank's running an office services agency, isn't he? Well surely the

75

businesses who need secretarial help will need it during ordinary working hours?'

'Oh no,' said Rose. 'It's quite different in war-time. Work goes on at all hours.'

Sally glanced at Uncle James again and this time caught a warning look from him.

'Oh well,' she said to Rose, 'I'll have plenty of chances to talk to Frank myself, so I'll stop pestering you now. Isn't it time I did something about that gas-mask?'

'I'll come with you,' said Rose. 'I'm not working in the office today.'

With a mingled feeling of relief and distress Sally allowed her sister to initiate her into the mysteries of life in wartime England, and Rose seemed to be equally glad to keep to safe topics. It was the first time in their lives that such a barrier had arisen between the sisters. Sally longed to explain to Rose that she was not in the least bit envious or resentful about the engagement, and that had Rose decided to marry a different sort of man she could have shared fully in Rose's joy. But any reference to Frank could only cause further strain, and so they talked of the blackout and the various National Defence leaflets as they went about their various errands, and the horror of the fall of Poland, and the publicity given to the fact that the King was to have the same rations as everybody else when rationing started. They might have been two strangers who had met on a tedious train journey or in a lengthy queue, and who were whiling away the time with the sort of chatter that was on everybody's lips.

It was late in the afternoon before they spoke of anything that was deeper in their hearts and minds. Rose had been buying groceries.

'There'll be five of us for a meal this evening,' she said, 'with Mother and you and Uncle James and Frank coming too.'

'Is Frank coming?' said Sally. 'I'm so glad. I'm really looking forward to meeting him, and perhaps he'll be able to give me advice about getting a job. I'd like to start work as soon as possible.'

It was an awkward peace offering on Sally's part, spoken with none of her normal directness and sincerity, but Rose clutched at it eagerly.

'He'll certainly be able to help you,' she said. 'He's in with all sorts of people – some of them quite high up in the Ministries. I'm sure you'll like him once you get to know him. And how about you, darling,' Rose hurried on, anxious perhaps that their little truce should not be put to too great a strain, 'when are you going to follow suit?'

Sally laughed. 'Never, I expect. I don't think I shall ever marry. Don't you remember my vow of celibacy when I'd decided to be a nun?'

'At the age of ten,' said Rose. 'I don't think you have to feel bound by that.'

'Ah, but it was terribly solemn! Mother and Dad were out that evening, and Nanny was asleep in the kitchen, and we went out on to the *stoep* in our nighties and looked at the stars, and I swore to the Southern Cross that I would devote my life to heavenly things.'

'And the week after that you were going to be the first woman to fly round the world. And the next one was an actress.'

'But never a housewife,' said Sally. 'I never had a daydream of being a respectable wife and mother.'

'Charlie Brent's been on the phone several times,' said

Rose. 'We told him we thought you'd be staying in Cape Town and we'd let him know when we heard from you. How about giving him a ring?'

'All right. I'll phone the infant Charles,' said Sally, with an indifference that was quickly and correctly interpreted by her sister.

'You've met someone else,' said Rose, stopping still on the pavement a few yards from the entrance to Park Mansions. 'In Cape Town or on the boat?'

'On the boat,' replied Sally with a grimace. 'That doesn't augur well, does it?'

'It depends,' said Rose assuming an air of wisdom and experience. 'There've been perfectly happy marriages of people who first met on a voyage.'

'A perfectly happy marriage is a contradiction in terms, and nothing is ever going to come out of this encounter. That's quite definite.'

Sally made a move to walk on. but Rose, persistent in a gently way, slowed down her step so that Sally was obliged to slow down too.

'What's he like?' asked Rose. 'Is he in London? Can I meet him?'

'I can't answer the first question' said Sally. 'I haven't the slightest idea what he's really like. The answer to the second question is yes, and to the third also, yes. I'd like you to meet him, but I'd like your first impressions without any prejudgement, so I won't say any more about him now.'

'Next week, then' said Rose pushing at the outermost of the swing doors that led to the foyer of Park Mansions. 'Let's get rid of Mother and Uncle James, and then we can do what we like.'

Chapter Seven

THE DINING-ROOM at No. 3 Park Mansions had originally been the maid's room. It led off the kitchen and was so small that there was only room for an oval table, six chairs and a narrow sideboard. With five people seated at table it felt very crowded, and Sally had had to steel herself to behave in an acceptable manner to Frank at such close quarters. But the meal turned out to be in some ways less of an ordeal than she had feared, because Mrs Livingstone's annoyance with her daughters dominated the dinner-table and left little room for other uncomfortable emotions.

'What my brother and I had hoped,' she said in a martyred voice to her prospective son-in-law, 'was that Rose would have come with me to Oxford and that you would join us whenever business allowed. But now, of course, Sally insists on staying in London, and Rose feels she ought to stay with her.'

Sally was so used to these blatant misrepresentations of the situation by her mother that this one barely touched her, but she noticed that Rose did not try to correct the impression given, and although Uncle James made one of his little throat-clearing noises nothing more came of it. It was plainly up to Frank to speak. He glanced at Sally before replying, and she looked straight at him, without a smile, but also without any hostility. There was the face, only a few feet away from her across the table, but her certainty of yesterday evening was gone, and she knew it could never be regained. Dr Christian Hofmeyr had done his work well, and Sally did not know whether to be grateful to him or to hate him for it. There had been terrible shock in that moment of certainty when she first saw Frank's face, but there had also been a grim kind of satisfaction in the possibility opened up of getting to the truth of the matter.

Had it not been for Chris, Sally was sure she would have told the whole story to Uncle James and they could have worked on it together, possibly even employing a private investigator to look into Frank Sedgemore's history. Between them they would surely have dug up enough hard facts either to confirm or disprove Sally's belief that he had been the man on the boat. At any rate there would have been facts, and she would not have been lost in this no-man's-land between doubt and certainty, a condition that she was beginning to find so intolerable that she feared it really could unsettle the balance of her mind. But then, had it not been for Chris, Sally reminded herself, she would never have brought the memory of that incident to the forefront of her mind at all, and it would have remained there, harsh and undigested, always ready to disturb and trouble and even threaten her. So really she was no worse off now than she had been before she told her story to Christian. As she reflected on this, Sally found herself clearly framing in her mind the question that she had been trying all day to suppress: was it conceivable that Christian himself had been the man on the boat, and had there been something deep in her buried self that had realized this and reacted by causing her to confide in him?

'But Oxford's only an hour's journey,' Frank Sedgemore was saying to Sarah Livingstone, 'and you'll be coming up and down to London too. I don't reckon we have to say a long farewell. As a matter of fact, it looks as if I might be having quite a bit of business to do in Oxford, so I'll be popping up there too.'

Sally jerked herself out of her own preoccupations and glanced at Uncle James. He was wiping his mouth with his table napkin, and he looked very red in the face.

'Business in Oxford!' cried Rose. 'But that's lovely. Why didn't you tell me before, Frank darling?'

'Because it only cropped up this afternoon,' he replied.

'Big deal?' said Sally brightly, unable to restrain herself although she was well aware that to talk of Frank's 'business' was to tread on dangerous ground.

'You could call it that,' he replied, turning to Rose and giving a slight wink, to which she responded with a delighted smile. 'But no shop at the dinner-table. That's the rule, isn't it. Madame Sarah?'

Mrs Livingstone began to melt a little.

'If you're going to be in Oxford, Frank,' she said, 'that makes a lot of difference. I shan't feel so much as if I've been banished into solitary exile. I expect you'll be needing somewhere to stay from time to time.' As she said this she looked at her brother, wondering if she dared suggest that there was room enough at Weir House for Frank to make it his *pied-à-terre*. Rose also looked at James Davenant with the same object in mind, but his face gave no encouragement to either of them to proceed. He helped himself to cheese and asked Sally to pass the butter.

'Oh, that won't present any problem,' said Frank in his easiest manner. 'I've several old pals in Oxford. They'll give me a bed all right, in return for services rendered.' Again he smiled at Rose and half-closed one eye. It was the eye the same side as the scar, and the wink and the broad smile had the effect of altering the shape of the face, so that Sally, looking at him and disliking him more every moment, at the same time found herself thinking that he looked less and less like the man on the boat. That he was dishonest and self-seeking she had no doubt at all. She was quite sure that he was involved in some unsavoury business now, and that he had probably been involved in many similar activities in the past, but that he had ever pushed a woman's body through a porthole into the Atlantic Ocean she was beginning to find more and more unlikely. He would not hesitate to get rid of somebody if he wanted to, she decided, but he would get someone else to do the actual dirty work for him, as no doubt he was getting Rose to do for him now, whatever the present dirty work might be. Whether Rose realized this or suspected it, Sally could not tell. Her own beloved sister had turned into a stranger, and every now and then the pain of it swelled up and overshadowed her other preoccupations.

After Frank's last remark nobody spoke for a while, all of them feeling, in their respective ways, something of the weight of James Davenant's silent gloom, though Sally alone felt sympathy with its cause. The silence was broken by the sound of the telephone ringing, and Sally, who was sitting nearest to the door, jumped up and ran down the passage to answer it.

'Can you talk?' asked Christian's voice.

'For a moment.'

'Have you found a job yet?'

'No.'

'Then here's a suggestion. The partnership deal is held up for the time being, but my colleague is starting up a temporary and very informal psychiatric guidance clinic in a house he's just taken in North London. He says there's plenty of provision for patching up broken bodies, but the minds upset by war are neglected – those of children and adults alike. He's raised a bit of money, and has the support of probation officers and other professional groups. We need someone to write the letters and keep the records and answer the phone and plug all the gaps. There'll be a little remuneration. Not much. Are you interested, Sally?'

'I'd love to do it!' cried Sally with great sincerity, and with a great upsurge of relief. If Chris could involve himself in such a worthwhile scheme as this, then he must be all right at heart, and the air of mystery surrounding him must be innocent in character, without any sinister content. Perhaps he had had a great and scarring loss; perhaps he himself had been through a severe mental illness. At any rate, if they were to work closely together she must surely get to know him better. The tensions of the family meal fell away from her; even the estrangement from her sister seemed to bite less deeply as Sally said again, 'I'd love to. When do we start?'

'Nine o'clock tomorrow morning. Come to my place first and I'll take you round to Ralph's and tell you more about it on the way. Any developments about the other business?' he added casually, almost as an afterthought.

'Nothing definite. Just a few impressions. I'll tell you when I see you. Have to go now. Goodbye.'

Sally put down the receiver and turned round to find herself face to face with Frank.

'Aha. An assignation,' he said with his knowing look. 'A very important assignation. But never fear.' He put a finger to his lips. 'Your secret is safe with me. Isn't it, honey?'

'What secret?' asked Rose, coming along from the kitchen with a tray of coffee cups.

'It's no secret at all,' said Sally irritably. 'I've just arranged to meet someone tomorrow morning about a possible job, that's all.'

'But Frank's going to find you a job.' Rose sounded as annoyed as her good temper ever allowed her to be. 'We talked about it.'

'We mentioned it, but we arranged nothing,' retorted Sally.

'Ladies, ladies!' cried Frank, slipping in between them and taking the coffee tray from Rose. 'Compose yourselves. What is a job? A trifling matter. Not worth the breath of argument. Of course I'd be glad to help, darling,' he said to Rose as they all moved in the big sitting-room, 'but if Sally has ideas of her own . . . war work maybe. Sister Sally sewing shirts for soldiers . . .'

'I think it was Sister Susie,' said Rose, smiling at him, and Sally turned her back on them for a moment and grimaced at the heavy blackout curtains and said to herself: damn him, damn him, under pretence of smoothing things over he's actually driving further in the wedge between us. Let them get on with it, but I'm still going to find out about him, whatever the outcome.

'Who was that on the phone, Sally?' asked Mrs Livingstone, coming into the room with Uncle James close behind her.

'A man I met on the boat,' replied Sally, turning to face them all and speaking firmly and clearly. 'A South African doctor who works in London and has offered me a job as a receptionist for a clinic he's starting up with a colleague.'

This remark produced quite a little sensation, with predictable reactions from the others present.

'Doctor, eh?' said Uncle James. 'Trained in England?'

'Scotland, I believe,' said Sally, having no grounds for this statement except a vague impression that Chris had once said something about one of the great Scottish medical schools. Uncle James gave one of his thoughtful grunts, which Sally interpreted as meaning that he was reserving judgement but was inclined to be favourable. Meanwhile Sally's mother was bombarding her with questions, and Rose said nothing, but gave Frank an affectionate and knowing look, to which he responded in kind. Sally noticed it, and heartily wished she had not mentioned Chris to Rose at all.

'I don't know much about him' she said to her mother. 'We only got to know each other during the last few days of the voyage. He told me he was interested in psychological medicine and had a colleague with whom he might be going into partnership.'

'H'm.' Uncle James's grunt was slightly less favourable. 'Don't know why they have to go in for that sort of thing. What the matter with good old-fashioned medicine?'

'You want to be careful of these trick cyclists, Sal,' said Frank. 'They're mostly crackers themselves.'

Sally very nearly burst out with an indignant 'Don't call

me Sal,' but managed to bite it back. 'It takes a long and hard professional training to qualify in psychological medicine,' she said coldly. 'Personally I find in very interesting, and also very relevant. There'll be plenty of psychological casualties in this war, as well as physical ones.'

Again Frank and Rose exchanged a smile and a significant look, which infuriated Sally even further because it said so plainly: She really is smitten – hark at her quoting him! Mrs Livingstone then said that of course everybody's nerves were on edge because of the war, and for once Sally actually felt quite grateful to her mother. This feeling did not last long, however, because Sally's mother proceeded to ask what the doctor's name was, and Sally had no alternative but to reply.

'Hofmeyr, Hofmeyr,' repeated Uncle James. 'Sounds like one of those Boer names to me.'

'We had two Hofmeyrs in my form at school,' said Rose, belatedly coming to Sally's help. 'It's a common enough name in Cape Town, Uncle James. They were both English-speaking, and were learning Afrikaans along with the rest of us.'

'Is he an Afrikaner, Sally?' asked her mother.

'He's just a South African!' exploded Sally. 'Just like my Dad was! And what's the matter with that, for heaven's sake? You're talking as if anyone without an Anglo-Saxon name is bound to be a German spy. I never heard such beastly narrow-minded prejudice. Aren't we all in the war together? Aren't we all fighting the same thing?'

'I really don't know what I have done to deserve this,' said Sarah Livingstone, sitting down with a martyred air.

'I ask a perfectly polite question, and this is the treatment I get. Really, Sally, if you're going to go on like this I can't help wishing you *had* stayed in Cape Town. There's been nothing but argument and quarrelling ever since you arrived.'

'I wish to God I had stayed!' yelled Sally. 'If this is all the welcome I get in what I thought was my own home!'

And she rushed out of the room, shaking off Rose, who tried to hold her back, and ran along the passage to the big kitchen at the back of the flat, where she walked up and down, beating her fists together and biting her lips in an attempt to hold back the threatened flood. The tears did not come, but the boiling of emotions within her was beyond endurance; the whole flat, sealed in by the blackout curtains, seemed to be closing in on her as in a nightmare; one of the others might come along any moment and start to talk to her, and there was no hiding place.

With a little cry of distress Sally ran back to the front hall, put on a coat and picked up her handbag. She had not the slightest idea where she was going; she only knew that she could not stay in the flat for another moment. When the outer door of the block had swung shut behind her she stood for a moment on the step, struck still by the all-enveloping darkness. It felt both stifling and unnatural. This vast sprawling city, whose millions of peacetime lights brought dawn to the sky the whole night long, now lay like some monstrous ghost town in a horror film of the extinguishing of mankind.

Sally heard the door swing open behind her, took a step or two forward, and then stopped again. At this moment even the tension within the flat seemed preferable to the weight of the blackness in the world outside.

'Are you there, Sally?'

It was with great relief that she recognized Uncle James's voice. She stretched out a hand, touched his arm and clung to it. 'I thought I'd go for a walk, but I'm rather scared,' she said.

'I'll come with you. Got my torch.'

Sally heard a little click, and suddenly there was a small circle of light on the concrete entrance way.

'Don't use it more than necessary,' continued Uncle James, switching it off again and leading her forward. 'Batteries in short supply already. Like everything else. Probably disappeared into the black market.'

They walked along for a while without talking, Sally finding great comfort in the feel of the fine cloth of Uncle James's coat-sleeve. A few cars and buses went by, their dimmed headlights making temporary flickers in the gloom, and then, in a moment of complete silence, came a sudden loud howling, a jungle noise in this dark jungle city.

'Hyenas?' said Sally.

'Sounds like something of that tribe,' said Uncle James.

'I wonder if the animals in the Zoo prefer the blackout,' said Sally. 'You'd think it would be more natural for them than the light.'

A little later she said: 'I'm sorry I burst out like that.'

'That's all right, Sal. Overtired. Need a night's sleep. Soon put you right.'

'I've been thinking about the arrangement you suggested,' Sally went on, knowing that Uncle James wanted to talk about it, but also knowing that he found difficulty in starting on a serious discussion of their family affairs. 'I do definitely want to stay in London, and it looks as if this job I've been offered could be a useful stop-gap while I'm looking for something more permanent. And I really am interested in mental health and I'd like to learn something about psychology. It isn't all nonsense, Uncle. Look at all those cases of shell-shocked soldiers in the Great War. If they could help people like that it would be something, wouldn't it?'

James Davenant admitted that shell-shock was a very terrible thing. 'What's this doctor fellow like?' he asked. 'Decent sort of chap?'

'I think you'd probably like him,' she replied. 'He's quiet and polite and doesn't obtrude himself. In fact, if anything he's too reserved. We hardly know each other, but we very much enjoy talking together. This is no whirlwind romance, Uncle. Truly. You needn't worry about that. I'm interested in his work, and I'd like to get to know him better, that's all.'

And that, said Sally to herself as she spoke these last words, is perfectly true as far as it goes. For a moment she was very tempted to add the rest of the truth about her feelings on the subject of Chris, but decided that it was not wise to do so. First of all, they were so vague that she hardly knew how to put them into words, and secondly, it would only muddle Uncle James. The important thing at this moment was to seek his help over Frank. Later on, perhaps, depending on how things turned out, she would confide in him about Christian.

'So I'd like to stay here during the week and come to Oxford at weekends,' she continued, 'but I'm rather dreading being with Rose and Frank. I can't stand him, Uncle. I can see exactly what you mean. And I'm sure he's a crook. If only we could get Rose to see it.'

'No use rushing things,' said Uncle James, holding tight to Sally's arm to save her from tripping after she had taken an unwary step off the edge of the pavement. 'That's the trouble with you youngsters. Always have to rush at things. Never stop to think them over.'

'You were young once, Uncle James,' said Sally. 'I'm sure you weren't always such a model of patience.'

'When I was your age,' he replied, 'the old Queen died, and it felt as if the world had come to an end. She'd been there so long that hardly anybody could remember a time when she hadn't been Queen. We felt as if nothing would ever be the same again. And nor it was. First the South African war, and then the Great War, and then nothing but troubles and that little madman raving away and everybody cringing and cowering for fear of what he'd do next. So here we are again. And what use was your League of Nations and all your Disarmament Conferences and all the rest of the pow-wow?'

'But they had to try!' cried Sally. 'Even if you haven't much hope of succeeding you still have to try.'

'I suppose so, I suppose so. But you'll never change human nature, you know, although other things—'

Uncle James broke off and they both recoiled as a light suddenly flared in front of them, a match struck to light a cigarette. They had a brief glimpse of a man's face, young and smooth and very intent on its little task, and in the dimmer outer circle of the light from the match they could see the pale blue airman's uniform.

'Let's go home, Sally,' said Uncle James. 'I don't think you'll find your mother will trouble you any more tonight. I expect you'll get your wish,' he went on as they reversed their steps. 'You'll see plenty of changes in this society of ours that you dislike so much. Always supposing we manage to come through this war. Otherwise . . .'

His voice faded away.

'Otherwise we go the way of Czechoslovakia and Poland,' said Sally. 'I don't think I want to think about it. In fact, I'm sure the only thing to do is not to think about it.'

'Exactly. Even if you haven't much hope of succeeding you still have to try. As you have just said yourself,' he added, and they both laughed a little.

Then Sally said: 'Well, even if we can't stop Hitler's tanks, you and I, we might at least be able to do something about Frank Sedgemore. I'm sure you're right and that his office agency is only a facade. What do you think he's really up to, Uncle James?'

'Black market,' replied James Davenant shortly. 'Building up large supplies of goods to release at outrageous prices later on when we really begin to suffer shortages.'

'That's it! That's him exactly,' cried Sally. 'I bet he's in league with Mother. That's why she loves him. But what about Rose? Does she suspect?'

'I don't know,' replied Uncle James unhappily. 'She must know something. Perhaps she doesn't understand how wrong it is.'

'Perhaps that's it,' said Sally without much conviction. 'Rose always liked having lots of nice clothes and people making a fuss of her,' she went on, half-regretfully and half-apologetically. 'But there's nothing wrong in that. You're always giving her presents and making a fuss of her yourself. And of me, too, of course,' she added a trifle belatedly.

'If this war goes on for a long time,' said James Davenant,

'and personally I believe it will, in spite of all those optimists who are cheerfully predicting that it will be over by the spring, then there are going to be plenty of things that I won't be able to give to you or to Rose. Things that money can't buy. Or that it ought not to be able to buy.'

'But she can't be planning to – I mean, surely Rose wouldn't be looking ahead like that. She's never been a calculating sort of person. She just likes nice things. Oh no. I won't believe it. Rose really loves him and admires him. Mother may be all over Frank because she thinks he'll supply her if things get short, but not Rose. Oh no, Uncle. Please not Rose.'

Sally's voice was very distressed. James Davenant patted the hand that clung to his sleeve.

'Course not,' he said. 'Rose is no schemer. She really loves the blighter.'

'I tell you what we are going to do,' said Sally presently in a much firmer voice. 'Don't be alarmed. We're not rushing it. We're going to work slowly and patiently. It's no use telling the police we suspect Frank, because I'm sure he's too clever to be caught, and that would only put Rose more and more on his side. We've got to show him up in a way that even Rose can't swallow. I've got a feeling I may have seen him before. I won't tell you about it now, because it's a long story and I may be quite wrong, but if I'm right, then he's even worse than a war profiteer, and we'll have to do something about it.'

Few people could have restrained themselves from asking questions after such a statement as this, but James Davenant was one of those few. He contented himself with begging Sally to be careful, and then asked if there was anything he could do to help.

'Yes,' said Sally promptly. 'You've got lots of contacts in the City. Do you know anyone who works in the Cape and County shipping offices? I want some detailed information on passenger lists and plans of boats. That sort of thing.'

'Bob Baines,' said Uncle James immediately. 'Used to be a director. Given up most of his directorships now – he's a good bit older than I am – but he knows them all in the offices. Ought to give him some sort of a reason for the inquiry, though.'

'Can't you have a niece who is a newspaper reporter writing a special article?'

Uncle James did not think that this would go down very well.

'A student, then. Doing research into the history of shipping.'

Students were apparently slightly less *persona non grata* than press people, but Sally could see that her uncle did not like this idea. She tried again. 'Suppose you tell him that I rather fancy myself as a writer of stories – after all, I did win that essay prize at school – and that I want to write a story based on my experiences on one of their ships and would like to have some convincing details.'

Sally herself thought this the most unconvincing of all the excuses she had suggested, but Uncle James seemed to think quite well of it.

'I'll try to fix something up,' he said, 'and perhaps you'll let me know what—'

'Ouch!' screamed Sally suddenly, interrupting him and holding even more tightly to his arm.

'Those darned sandbags,' grumbled Uncle James. 'Stubbed your foot?'

'And how!' Sally bent to rub it. 'I don't think that walks in the blackout are much fun. What are these sandbags doing on this corner anyway? There's no police station or fire station or anything. And surely they oughtn't to put them halfway across the pavement?'

'Another bit of bumbledom,' said Uncle James. 'I suppose we'll get used to that too in time. There's a ramshackle shed that's supposed to be an air-raid shelter here, but don't you two girls go near it. The roof's not properly protected. Get under the kitchen table if there's any trouble. It's good and solid, and will bear a lot of weight. That's your safest place in the flat. And keep away from glass. Deadly stuff, splintered glass.'

'Yes, that's what they told us on the boat,' said Sally. 'We had hours and hours of life drill and boat drill and taking-cover drill. I suppose it kept us occupied and made us feel a bit better, but I think we all knew in our hearts that it was pretty useless if we did get torpedoed. Didn't Mother worry about me at all?' added Sally almost pleadingly and in spite of herself. 'Didn't Rose?'

'Course they did,' replied James Davenant too heartily. 'Course they worried. There was hardly any news getting through, you know. Your mother asked me to keep in touch with the Cape and County offices, and I said all along that you might be on the *Rutlandshire*. They didn't agree. They were sure you'd cancel. Made 'em feel happier to believe you were safe in Cape Town, so I stopped arguing, but I still went on hoping. And I'm glad to have you home, Sal,' he concluded awkwardly.

Sally pressed his arm, and they returned to the flat in silence. For once she was glad of the darkness, because it hid the tears that were slowly forcing themselves out.

94

Chapter Eight

THERE WERE SOUNDS of merriment coming from the sitting-room of No. 3 Park Mansions. Frank, Rose and Mrs Livingstone were playing rummy, and as Sally and her uncle came into the room Rose turned round and called to them to join in.

'Come and help us cope with Frank,' she said, laughing and looking slightly flushed and very pretty. 'He's winning every game.'

Sally was longing to go to bed, but felt it was worth making a little sacrifice for the sake of the appearance of family harmony. At least the game gave her an opportunity to study Frank at close quarters but with less strain than there had been at the dinner table. He seemed to be making some sort of effort to be friendly to her, and she did her best to respond.

After playing another couple of rounds Rose and her mother decided it was time to make tea, and they went off to the kitchen together. Uncle James got up to switch on the wireless for the news, and stood in the far corner of the big room in front of the set, listening with his back to the others. Frank gave Sally one of his winks, and then leant forward and whispered: 'Are you a news-hound too?'

She showed her surprise but did not recoil from him.

'Personally I'm sick to death of it,' he said very quietly, but in the most straightforward and unaffected tones she had yet heard him use. 'People are glued to the wireless all day long, and it's mostly lies, anyway, dished up for us by Minny.'

'Minny?'

'Ministry of Information. They're the people who are running the country, believe me. I know some of them.'

I bet you do, thought Sally, but she was determined to make the most of this moment of contact with Frank, and she continued to lean forward and speak in a friendly manner under cover of the loud clear voice of the BBC announcer.

'I'd like to hear more about it some time,' she said. 'I expect there'll be a chance for us to get to know each other, but there's one thing I'm longing to ask – I hope you don't think I'm being awfully personal – but I can't help wondering how you got that scar.'

Frank touched his cheek and smiled. 'Not a war wound, I'm afraid. Nor even in a duel. Nothing so romantic. It's the remains of a bad smash-up I had about five years ago. Trying out a sporty little model for a pal. He thought it was a bargain for a used car, and so did I, till the brakes failed when I was doing ninety. I went through the windscreen, and was lucky to end up with no worse permanent damage.'

Sally made suitably sympathetic and interested noises. 'Where did it happen?' she asked. 'I shouldn't like to be driving at ninety miles an hour on any road I know.'

'Not far from Oxford. There's a good straight stretch of road they call Fair Mile. You may know it from the times you've stayed with your folks. Luckily there weren't any other cars involved. Just me hitting a tree and finishing up over the hedge in a bed of stinging nettles. Extraordinary thing, you know, Sal. I never lost consciousness, although I was bleeding like a pig, and I swear I suffered more from those damned nettles than from any of the injuries.'

'It sounds quite frightful,' said Sally smiling. He was speaking quite naturally, and there was no trace of the assumed transatlantic accent in his voice. He's just a Cockney boy living on his wits, she said to herself, whether or not it's true that he was born in India. For a moment she found that she almost liked him and did not even resent his calling her 'Sal.' At any rate, she said to herself, this accident is something that can easily be checked, and if it's all true, then the scar is more recent than the voyage on the *Cape St Vincent*, whether or not he was ever on that boat.

'Nothing new,' said Uncle James switching off the wireless and returning to his seat.

'There never is,' said Frank. 'If and when it ever happens to us we won't even know about it. We'll just cop it. Don't suppose those poor devils in Warsaw had a clue what was hitting them until it did.'

'D'you think the Russians will stay out of it now?' asked Sally. Frank had put on his knowing manner again as soon as Uncle James approached them, and her brief moment of liking for him was over.

'Heaven help us if they don't,' said Uncle James. 'Germany and Russia together, and nothing but us and the French to keep the balance. We're practically un-armed, thanks to the imbeciles who've been governing the country since the last war, and as for the French, they'll crumple up like paper if the going gets really rough. If only the Americans would come in, but I don't see much chance of that after Roosevelt's speech the other night.'

'The dear old Yanks,' said Frank, 'sitting on the sidelines as usual. We're ever so sorry for all you brave folks in the old country, and we'll throw you a few pennies now and then, but as for coming to help . . . Never mind, Sally. I don't think we need get too worried about the old Russkis. Hitler and Stalin – there's no honour among thieves there. They don't mix. No more than oil and water. With Poland finished I reckon we've seen the last of the Russo-German pact.'

Uncle James gave one of his grunts. Sally suspected that he agreed with Frank but could not bear to admit it. Dearly as she loved her uncle, she was beginning to think she would make more progress with Frank on her own, and it was a relief when the door opened and Rose and her mother came in with the tea.

'I suppose we ought to be going carefully with tea,' said Sally as she watched the dark liquid being poured into her cup, 'if it's going to be rationed.'

'I don't see that that's any reason for stinting ourselves now,' said Mrs Livingstone. 'Besides, Frank says we'll be all right, and I know we can trust Frank.'

And she gave him one of her melting looks, to which he responded, Sally thought, with a certain amount of embarrassment. Uncle James made some of his disapproving throat-clearing noises, and Sally quickly said, in a very friendly and innocent voice: 'What are you going to do, Frank? Give us your rations?'

There was more to be gained, she believed, by this line of approach than by letting Frank see that she was suspicious of him.

'That's right,' said Frank laughing. 'I'm going to give you my rations. Can't let three charming ladies go short, can we, beautiful?'

This last was addressed to Rose, who was looking very smug and pleased. Sally decided that she had done enough in the cause of present domestic harmony and future detective work, and that she deserved now to go to bed.

'I can't keep awake another minute,' she said standing up. 'Sorry. Good night all.'

As she left the room she heard a voice call out: 'Mind you get your beauty sleep for your charming doctor tomorrow.'

It was Rose's voice, not Frank's, and at that moment Sally felt an emotion that she would never before have thought possible. It was something like a feeling of hatred for her own dearest Rose. She fought it down, but it came back in the confusion of her dreams, where Rose's sweet complacent face mingled with that of the man on the boat, and with Christian's face in its heavy spectacles, and with the twisted raving maniac face of Adolf Hitler.

Sally woke from these dreams to find Rose standing by the bedside with a cup of tea. The impression of the dream lingered, giving an air of sinister mystery to Rose in her pale blue dressing-gown.

'I didn't want to wake you,' she said, 'but it's a quarter to eight, and you did say you wanted to be up early.'

'I was dreaming about you,' said Sally sitting up and taking the teacup, 'and you looked like Hitler.'

Rose made a face, and then laughed as she left the room. But it's all wrong between us, thought Sally, and it will never be right again, whatever happens about Frank.

Was it Rose who had changed, or did the change lie in herself? Was she really going through some phase of mental and nervous unbalance, brought on by digging up that memory of the *Cape St Vincent* voyage? Surely it was not normal to keep having these fits of seeing people and things in this strange way – Rose as Hitler, Frank as the murderer on the boat, and Chris . . .

What was Chris? Sally asked herself as she dressed. An interesting, intelligent, and companionable man whom she was very keen to know better? Or some dark, threatening force that had come into her life at a crucial moment and was manipulating her in the manner of a Svengali?

Well, at least Uncle James is the same as he always was, thought Sally, as she joined him at the kitchen table for breakfast; I'm not mixing him up with some monster, and Mother is just the same, too. These reflections comforted her, and when she met Christian as arranged at the front door of the house where he lived she told him briefly about this curious double-vision of hers, and ended by saying laughingly that she was still having frightful rows with her mother, which must surely be a sign of sanity.

'You are completely sane,' said Chris with unusual warmth in his voice. 'Very sane and very intelligent and very—'

He broke off suddenly.

'I only wish—', he began and broke off again.

Sally turned to look at him as they walked along and believed she saw in his face more signs of emotion than she had yet seen in him, and she was conscious of a little flurry of excited anticipation, as in the hush before the rising of the curtain at a play, or the moment before the hawsers are loosed and the voyage begins.

'I'm sorry,' said Christian. 'I don't think I can tell you any more just yet. Perhaps one day. Just let me say how very great a respect and admiration I have for you and let me assure you that I am indeed your friend, although perhaps you may find it difficult—'

Yet again he stopped in the middle of a sentence.

'I can see you're finding it difficult to talk,' said Sally. 'I can't deny that you've got me bursting with curiosity, but if it's something you don't feel able to tell me now then let's leave it alone for the time being. I'm very grateful to you for your high opinion of me and I do indeed believe that you are my friend. How quaint we must sound,' she added laughingly. 'Like characters from an old-fashioned novel!'

'Let me tell you about Ralph Curtis,' said Christian. 'We'll be there in a minute, and I've been wasting the time. We were at school together in Cape Town and both always wanted to be doctors, though we went to different medical schools, both for our general training and for our diploma in psychological medicine. He's quite a different type of character from myself. Very extrovert. I daresay you'll find him delightful. Most women do. He ought to have been well on the way to being a consultant by now, but unfortunately he drinks rather a lot, and on more than one occasion it has endangered his career. If we can get into practice together I'll be able to keep an eye on him and I'm hoping to prevent any more of such incidents. He's very good at his job and it would be a wicked waste if he had to give it up. You don't say anything, Sally. I'm afraid

I've prejudiced you against poor Ralph. But you'd have guessed for yourself, and I had to tell you.'

'I don't much like doctors who drink too much,' said Sally. 'Nor anyone else who does, for that matter. But I can't say any more till I've met him, except that I think you are a very loyal friend.'

'It's not all one-sided. He pulled me though a bad patch after my marriage broke up. And he's helped me financially. He's putting up the money to start his emergency clinic, but we'll need to raise more if it's to be a success. I hope you'll help in that. Here we are.'

They had been walking northwards, away from the immediate neighbourhood of Regent's Park, and had reached an area of big and dingy Victorian terraces, with crumbling porticos and no flowers or greenery to be seen except some neglected geraniums in the window-box of a basement flat. Albert Place was a wide street, but there was little traffic, and a group of children were kicking a ball backwards and forwards across the roadway, screaming and shouting, and sometimes attacking each other quite viciously.

'I thought they were all supposed to be evacuated to safe areas,' said Sally.

'Apparently some of them have managed to get themselves lost and are literally running wild,' said Chris, 'and some whole families have come back already because they were so bored in the country.'

He pulled at an old-fashioned bell-rope beside one of the shabbier doorways. Surprisingly, it worked, and the door was opened by a man of medium height and stocky build with fair hair and deep blue eyes and a very pink complexion. Sally's first thought was one of relief that this was not another possible candidate for the man on the boat. Nobody could have looked more unlike him than Dr Ralph Curtis, and in her present state of doubt and suspicion, both about herself and about others, it was a comfort to be sure of this one fact at least.

'Miss Livingstone?' he said holding out a hand. 'Chris told me about you. Do come in. I'm afraid the place is in a frightful mess. I've only just moved in, and it has been uninhabited for some months. There used to be a doctor's surgery here at one time,' he added leading them along a passage and opening the door on a fair-sized room with a wash-basin in the corner, 'so the basic facilities aren't too bad. Not that it matters so much if we're going to be doing mainly psychiatric work. This little cubby-hole –' and he pushed open another door – 'seems to have been used as the receptionist's office, so if you think you can manage in here, Miss Livingstone . . . I'm afraid it's hardly up to luxury office block standard.'

'I don't mind where I work,' said Sally. 'I'll type in the bathroom if there's nowhere else. When do we open for business?'

'Well, actually,' said Dr Curtis glancing at his watch, 'the Probation Officer is bringing someone along at eleven. It's a fifteen-year-old girl who keeps running away from home because—' He broke off and glanced at Christian before continuing. 'It's rather a sordid case, I'm afraid, Miss Livingstone. I hope you don't mind.'

'Sally's not squeamish,' said Christian. 'She won't mind typing clinical case reports dealing with rape or incest or whatever it is that's worrying you, Ralph. She's here to do a job, and wants to be treated like a colleague and not a piece of porcelain. That's right, isn't it, Sally?'

'Of course,' said Sally feeling grateful to Chris, but at the same time feeling awkward because she didn't know what he had told his friend about her. Was she just the girl he had met on the *Rutlandshire*? Or had he told Ralph her own story? Sally felt that this was unlikely, but nevertheless she felt uncomfortable under Dr Curtis's appraising look, and determined to ask Chris about it at the first possible opportunity.

The chance did not come until late in the afternoon. By the time they had inspected the rest of the accommodation and drawn up a rough plan of action the Probation Officer had turned up with not only one probem adolescent but two, and both Chris and Ralph became absorbed in lengthy interviews while Sally tried out Ralph's portable typewriter, found some paper on which to take notes should she be required to do so, and did a bit of cleaning in the kitchen, which was very dirty. After that she felt rather at a loss and was very tempted to go upstairs and explore Dr Curtis's living quarters. He had actually shown her his bathroom and lavatory on the first floor and told her to use them in preference to the antiquated one in the surgery area, but Sally was afraid she would not be able to resist looking into the other rooms too. And when I go exploring, she said to herself, I tend to come across things like men pushing bodies out of portholes. But after all, she continued with her argument, I have got some detective work on hand. Chris is part of the mystery. I've just learnt for the first time that he once had a wife, and now I've met his best friend. And this house is his friend's.

She put her ear to the keyhole of first one and then the other of the closed doors on the ground floor. Both consultation sessions seemed to be in full swing. On the first floor all the doors were open. Sally used the bathroom, and then looked into the two rooms that were furnished as a bedroom and a sitting-room respectively. There were crates of books standing on the floor of the latter, and the general appearance was of a place where someone had only just moved in.

The furniture, carpet and curtains were of much better quality than the nondescript contents of Christian's flat, and stacked against the wall were some pictures of South African scenes by an artist whose name Sally recognized as having achieved a considerable reputation in Cape Town. Dr Ralph Curtis was obviously a man of some substance, though presumably he had bought or rented the house very cheaply, owing to the collapse of the property market in war-time London.

Pity if all these nice things got bombed, thought Sally as she moved across to a light mahogany bureau-book-case, the desk part of which was open and covered with letters and documents in a state of great disorder. Sally stood for a moment, debating whether she would be justified in actually reading anything, but was saved from having to make the decision by the sound of a door opening on the floor below, and of voices in the hall. Her eyes had noted only one detail of the contents of the desk before she moved away. It was an ivory paper-knife, with a wide blade, and a handle carved in a scroll design enclosing some elaborate initials. She had noticed it because it was exactly the same as a paper-knife that her mother had once given to her father, except that his initials had been FRL, and those cut into the ivory knife on Dr Curtis's desk were RCH.

Ralph Curtis? But why the H, wondered Sally as she ran

downstairs and found that the callers were all departing and that she and the two doctors were to go out and have some lunch.

'Nothing but workmen's dives round here,' said Ralph, 'but I've got the car now, and it won't take ten minutes to run up to Hampstead to my favourite hostelry.'

'What about the petrol ration?' asked Sally, feeling sure that she was going to like neither Ralph's driving nor his idea of a pleasant meal.

'Doctors are privileged people,' he replied, giving her a sort of knowing smile that reminded her of Frank Sedgemore.

The bar turned out to be crowded and uncomfortable and full of loud upper-class voices. Ralph drank a lot more than he ate, and Sally noticed that Chris looked anxious. The relationship between the two of them puzzled her more and more. Men can be very odd in their friendships and loyalties, she said to herself, but there seemed something more than just this oddness in the attitudes of these two men to each other. It was as if they needed each other. Or rather, since Chris seemed to Sally to be as self-sufficient a person as she had ever met, as if each of them had some sort of hold over the other that was keeping them linked together.

Perhaps they're partners in crime, she thought as Ralph drove them much too quickly back to the house. After all, there were plenty of profitable and illegal activities that an unscrupulous doctor could indulge in. Performing surgery on notorious criminals to make them unrecognizable, for instance. Charles Brent, in one of their nonsense conversations, had once expounded on the theme of being personal medical adviser to a big-time gangster like Al Capone. Sally told herself that she was being absurd in her imaginings; and in fact, the afternoon's activities put an end to suspicions of this kind, at least for the time being. Whatever these two had done in the past or were planning to do in the future, there was no doubt that the present emergency psychiatric clinic scheme was both genuine and necessary. They dictated long letters and reports on the morning's cases, and Sally found the afternoon hours going by in a flash. Ralph then started talking about their making a foursome for the evening with a girl he knew, but to Sally's great relief Chris turned this down.

'I'm sorry you don't like Ralph,' he said as they walked away together.

'I like the way he works,' said Sally. 'I think he was marvellous with that girl who's suddenly turned violent. D'you think it's this awful waiting – being at war and yet nothing happening? D'you think people will feel better if we do start being bombed?'

Chris laughed. 'Yes, I think they probably will. The reality is so often less bad than the fear of it.'

'In that case perhaps I ought to go and jump off Westminster Bridge to get rid of my fear of looking down on water,' said Sally.

'If you're a good enough swimmer it might not be a bad idea, though I don't think you'd enjoy all the commotion and attention you'd attract.'

'Then I'll do it somewhere less public. I know. I'll practise by the weir near Uncle James's home when we go there for weekends. It's been one of my worst horror places since we came to live in England. The river splits in two at their village, and it's the deepest lock on the

107

Thames on one branch of it, and this perfectly horrible rushing water on the other. You can walk across it on a narrow bridge, and the times I've had to make excuses for Uncle to take us for a walk in the other direction!'

'I think you'd better be careful, Sally,' said Christian. There was something in his voice that made Sally slow her step and glance up at him. On the sombre face was an expression that she could not fathom. Was it tenderness? Was it concern? Whatever it was, it made her heart beat more quickly, and she caught her breath. But it's no use feeling like this, she told herself, walking on again. I've got to get to the bottom of the mystery about him before there can be anything between us, and if he doesn't feel he can tell me . . .

'I'll be careful,' she said. 'I'm beginning to understand my phobia better, thanks to you. Did you tell Ralph about me, by the way? About that man on the *Cape St Vincent*, I mean.'

Sally looked at Christian again as she asked this question, and she had the feeling that there was a very slight hesitation, as if he was switching over from an open and spontaneous reaction to a more restrained one before he replied.

'None of the detailed circumstances. Only that you had this fear that seemed to date from a childhood trauma. I told him in detail what I thought about you, though,' he added, reverting to the warmth of manner, 'and now he's seen for himself. You've worked like a Trojan today, but I don't want you to feel obliged to put in so many hours every day. You must have time off to look for a permanent job and attend to your own affairs as well.'

For the rest of the walk they discussed the clinic, but

108

just before they parted Sally asked as casually as she could: 'Have you got another name, Chris? One that you don't use? My second name is Angelina. After my grandma. Isn't it awful?'

'My first one is as bad. Rudolph. I never use it.'

'I don't blame you. See you tomorrow afternoon then, Chris.'

'Three o'clock. Not a minute earlier. And try to have a restful morning.'

'With Mother starting the packing for the move to Oxford for the duration? The flat will be chaos. I'll probably go and call on some friends.'

Rudolph, repeated Sally to herself as she walked across the park in the evening sunlight, barely glancing now at the silver barrage balloons, so quickly had they lost their novelty and become part of her normal environment. Rudolph Christian Hofmeyr. RCH. The initials on the ivory paper-knife now in the possession of Dr Ralph Curtis. Well, they had been at school together and were old friends. Perhaps they had lent or given each other some of their possessions from time to time.

Chapter Nine

THE LONDON OFFICES of the Cape and County Line were in a narrow alleyway leading off Ludgate Hill, in the shadow of St Paul's Cathedral. Sally had been there once or twice in connection with her own recent travellings, and she recognized the elderly clerk who received callers and dealt with straightforward enquiries. He and his colleagues at the neighbouring desk greeted her kindly and asked questions about the voyage on the SS *Rutlandshire*. When Sally explained her present errand, the way was made smooth for her. Uncle James had been in touch with Bob Baines, who in his turn had sent the message down the hierarchy that Miss Sally Livingstone was to be given all the information she required.

Sally was taken through the large and gloomy general office to an inner room that was smaller, but no less dismal. The only window was plastered over with strips of paper to protect it from bomb blast, and the one central light hung low under a plain green shade and shone only on the desk, leaving much of the room shadowy. An even more elderly man, who was introduced as Mr Bainbridge, got up from behind the desk and fussed over Sally, very concerned that she should have a chair that was comfortable for her and that she should not be either too hot or in a draught. He seemed so bent and frail himself that she felt as if she ought to be the one who was doing the fussing, and she found herself more and more disliking the sort of part Uncle James had advised her to play in this male stronghold. It was obvious, though, that the best way to get what she wanted had been to dress up a bit, borrowing a new and fashionably tilted hat from Rose that made her look more like the city man's idea of a leisured young society lady, and not the passionate seeker after truth that she felt herself to be.

'What I wondered, Mr Bainbridge,' she said, 'was whether I could see a plan of the *Cape St Vincent*. I suppose another ship would do if you haven't got one, but it would be rather nice if you have, because that was the first ship I ever travelled on and I'll never forget that voyage.'

And that is true, at least, thought Sally, producing a beaming smile that partly arose from ironic amusement with her own acting.

'I do hope I'm not interrupting you too much,' she added. 'It's awfully good of you to spare the time to satisfy my curiosity when you must be terribly busy.'

'Not at all, not at all, I'm not at all busy, and it's a pleasure to help you,' said Mr Bainbridge. 'I've got the *Cape St Vincent* here.' He turned to one of the big dark cabinets and pulled papers out of a long drawer. 'Here she is. Poor old *Vincent*. She was broken up for scrap ten years ago. That must have been her last voyage, the one you mention. It can't have been very comfortable. She used to roll dreadfully. I once went out to the Cape in her myself.'

'It wasn't very comfortable,' said Sally as Mr Bain-

111

bridge spread the plans over the desk and they bent over them together. 'I was seasick practically all the time, except when we stopped at Tenerife for the day.'

'Ah yes. Tenerife. Colourful spot. Always feel as if you're not far from home once you get to Tenerife, although the worst of the voyage is usually still to come.'

'You've done it a number of times, then' said Sally, and took the opportunity to look closely at the plans, while Mr Bainbridge broke out into reminiscence.

C Deck, she said to herself. That's where our cabin must have been. Port side. How tiny and crowded it all looks on the plan. But it really was tiny and crowded. That's right. There's the bathroom. And one in the same place the other side of the ship. In the curve of the bows. And the stairs right in the middle. It really was quite isolated down there, with everyone upstairs jollifying.

'That's where we travelled, down on C Deck in the second-class,' she said when Mr Bainbridge paused for a moment.

'Oh dear, that can't have been at all pleasant for you, Miss Livingstone,' said the old clerk. 'Even the first-class accommodation on some of those old boats left much to be desired, while as for the steerage . . .'

His voice trailed away, and Sally, glancing at the weak pale eyes and the wrinkled papery complexion of the old man, suddenly felt a twist of pity in her heart for all humanity. He'll have travelled steerage, she thought; he'll always have had to make do with the cheapest and the worst. And climbing ever so slowly up the ladder of promotion; and always having to kowtow to those above; and having to be polite and deferential to gentry like me; and getting older and older and more and more tired; and working becoming more and more of an effort and nothing to look forward to . . .

Suddenly she had an impulse to take Mr Bainbridge by both hands and smile at him and say: 'Never mind. Try not to mind. Your life has been narrow and dreary and others have been much worse, but it won't always be like that . . . there'll come a day when we'll all be the same . . . when nobody is superior to anybody else . . . when everyone has a right to a full and open life . . . to be really themselves . . .'

The impulse faded. You're a fool, Sally Livingstone, she told herself. He's probably got a nice little nest-egg tucked away somewhere and is perfectly content with his life, and anyway you're here on business and had better get on with it.

'Where did the stewards and stewardesses work from?' she said aloud. 'I can't see anywhere on C deck.'

'No. They'd be up here.' Mr Bainbridge's finger moved to another part of the plan. 'This little red bit. That's the pantry.'

'What a lot of running about they must have had to do,' said Sally.

'Yes indeed. Terrible conditions for the crew there were on those old boats. They had a lot to put up with. Oh dear.' The elderly clerk looked quite frightened for a moment. 'I ought not to have said that.'

'Don't worry about me, I won't repeat it.' Sally smiled at him again. 'In fact the more low-down you can give me the happier I shall be.' She was about to add that it would add colour to the story she was writing, the story that was the excuse for her seeking information from the shipping line, but she had a feeling that Mr Bainbridge had already forgotten about this excuse for her visit, and was enjoying talking to her and would be happy to go on talking. His reaction proved that she was right in this assumption.

'Poor old *Cape St Vincent*,' he said, running his finger over the paper with an almost tender touch. 'She was a sister ship of the *Cape Agulhas*, the last two of the old Cape Line before the merger with the County. I was with the old Cape Line, you know, Miss Livingstone. Started as an office boy when I was twelve. We went to work young in those days. And when the merger came they took me over too.' He smiled in a way that once again caused Sally to feel that little tug at the pathos of humanity. 'But they didn't send me to the scrap-heap straight away. Gave me a little job in the new offices and let me think I was being useful.'

'I'm sure you were being useful!' cried Sally, who was beginning to think she would burst into tears if this went on much longer. 'And you're being very useful to me now, Mr Bainbridge. Do tell me more about the *Cape St Vincent*. Could passengers get through easily from one class to another – say from first to second or from second to first? It doesn't look as if there's any way through on the lower decks. How about up top?'

'Ah, that was the trick,' said the old man with a chuckle. 'You climbed up from the well-deck where the second-class passengers sometimes used to sit, up on the boat deck. Not really encouraged, of course, but the crew always turned a blind eye on courting couples. And from there you went down into the first. Easy enough once you knew the way.'

Sally bent over the plans again. 'Yes, I see,' she said at last. 'Why, that's where I must have been sitting – up there on the boat deck – when that nice steward came and talked to me and told me how to avoid being so sick! He was very kind. I've never forgotten him.'

'Now I wonder who that could have been,' said Mr Bainbridge. 'Deck steward in the second-class of the *Cape St Vincent*. Let me see, now. They would have the old lists over in the staffing department, but perhaps I can find something for you here . . . let me see, I've got the passenger lists, of course – it's my job, you see, to look after the records of the company, Miss Livingstone, just in case anybody wants to write a history of it one day, but there are gaps. Very big gaps, I'm afraid. People are sometimes very careless with papers, and office staff are not what they used to be. I'd like to find out for you who was your friend on the boat deck, but I'm not sure if I've got any records of the crew at that time. I'll have a look.'

'May I see the passenger lists while you're looking?' asked Sally, who could still hardly believe that it was all turning out so easy. 'I'd like to see our names. I suppose my mother had one at the time, but you don't know about these things when you're a child, and she never keeps any letters or papers.'

Mr Bainbridge went to another of the filing cabinets, produced a folder, and placed it on the desk, and then proceeded to turn over its contents so slowly and deliberately that Sally hardly knew how to restrain her impatience. Her heart was beating quickly, and her breathing was speeding up as well. She felt as if she would burst if she didn't get a quick sight of that list to see whether there were any familiar names on it apart from that of Livingstone.

'Shall I look, Mr Bainbridge?' she asked as calmly as

she could. 'If you're sure it's in this file, I can find it for myself while you look for the names of the crew. I can't help you with that, since I've no idea where they might be.'

She smiled at him again, and he yielded up the folder and retreated to the darkest corner of the room and began to rummage in the cupboard that stood there. Sally was glad that he had his back to her and that she had no need to control the expression on her face. Preventing herself from crying out was difficult enough. She found the lists in no time, and her quick eye instantly scanned them for names that she knew. In the second-class were the three Livingstones and no other name that meant anything to her. In the list of first-class passengers was included a Hofmeyr, R. C. There was no sign of a Sedgemore anywhere.

But I suppose Frank could have used a false name, thought Sally; or perhaps this one is false. Or he could have been a member of the crew. Even as she thought this, however, she had the feeling that this was not the solution. Deep within her was growing the conviction that Frank Sedgemore had never been on the *Cape St Vincent*, that the story of how he got his scar was going to be confirmed beyond all doubt, and that the extraordinary flash of recognition that had occurred to her when she first saw him was indeed a mirage of her own imagination, created by tension and exhaustion and over-strained nerves, and the fact that she had earlier that day for the first time in years allowed the memory of what she had seen on the boat really to come to the front of her mind. The sight of anybody resembling the man she had seen would have had that effect on her. Frank Sedgemore had

116

resembled him, and the scar had enormously reinforced the impression. And later on she had disliked Frank so much that she wanted him to turn out to be a murderer.

Later evidence might prove her wrong, but as Sally sat staring at the open file in the dim and dusty office, she had an overwhelming impression that in Christian lay the heart of the mystery.

R. C. Hofmeyr. Among the first-class passengers. There could be other men of that name, of course. A common enough name, as Rose had pointed out. But the initials were right, and Chris had travelled on those old boats and had once spent Christmas at sea. Somehow or other he had avoided saying on what voyage, but he must surely know that Sally would take the first opportunity to investigate for herself.

And he had deliberately put himself forward as a candidate for the man on the boat. It looked now as if that had been done as a very bold measure, designed to discover whether or not she would recognize him. And because her head had been so full of Frank at the time she had not recognized Christian as the man . . .

Sally glanced up and saw the bent shoulders and the sparse grey hair of the old clerk as he continued to search in the cupboard in the corner. Her thoughts raced on. The scar. Chris had no scar. Or hadn't he? The glasses he wore had very thick rims, and she had never seen him without them. The scar was high on the cheekbone, under the eye socket. Could it possibly be that the lower rim of the glasses was hiding it? And then there was the fact that he had wanted to tell her something but had said he could not. Was it a confession? He had looked so unlike his usual confident self;

he had spoken so warmly to her. Surely he could not be guilty.

But how could he be not guilty? And how could there be anything more between them once she had proved that he was?

Sally felt as if her mind was being torn in two. She felt it as a physical pain, as if she herself was being made the object of a tug-of-war. Such a condition could not be endured for long; she felt herself being pulled over to the other side, and her thoughts began racing away in the other direction. She was making a terrible mistake, of course. Christian was totally innocent. He was a good and honourable man with great abilities and determined to use them for the good of humanity . . . just such a man as Sally could like and respect, and since he had shown how much he liked and respected her, he might well be just such a man as she could truly love . . . and a man whom she could truly love was someone out of the ordinary, because she did not love easily, and was cynical and critical beyond her years . . .

'Ah! Here it is.'

Sally gave a start at the sound of these words. Her mind had shot off into a dream of a life with Chris, sharing all his interests and concerns, which were so much her own, and she had momentarily forgotten Mr Bainbridge.

'What have you found?' she managed to ask after a moment's hesitation.

'It's the captain's farewell party. That was the last voyage of the *Cape St Vincent*, just as I thought, and Captain Hudson gave a party for his old friends among the crew. He was very popular, and many of them had been with him for years. He kept a record of it all – there you are.'

Mr Bainbridge produced a thick exercise book with a stiff navy-blue cover.

'It's his personal diary – not a ship's log. He always liked to think of himself as a writer and planned to make it his retirement hobby.'

'It's a beautiful handwriting,' said Sally, turning over the pages of the exercise book. 'I don't remember him at all from the boat – but then I was only a child and I was ill all the time. Where does he live now?'

As she asked this question her mind was already busy with a meeting with Captain Hudson. Surely Uncle James would be able to arrange it, and surely if anyone knew what had been going on aboard that boat, it would be the captain.

'He doesn't live anywhere,' said Mr Bainbridge. 'He died of pneumonia six months after he retired. We were all very sad. He was a great gentleman, Captain Hudson.'

Sally was conscious of a strange mixture of disappointment and relief. Her mind was beginning to split in two again. She wanted to find out the truth, and yet she did not want to know. Or rather, she only wanted to know what Chris himself chose to tell her. But if he were to tell her anything she knew she would still not believe it. That was no way out of her dilemma. The only way was to find out for herself, to hear the evidence from somebody whose word was above suspicion, somebody like Captain Hudson.

'Here are the pages covering his goodbye party,' said Mr Bainbridge. 'You see he has been very careful to note both the name and the position in every case. George Cunningham – he was purser. He retired at the same time and went back to live in Cape Town. Quite a number of them did – the older ones I mean. Let's see if we can find your deck steward. If he was getting on in years he'd have been with Captain Hudson for a long time and he'd surely have been invited . . . Ah, here we are.'

Mr Bainbridge's fingers came to rest near the bottom of a page. 'Albert Harrington. That will be your man.' I can't tell you anything about him myself, but we can find out whether he transferred to another ship or whether he retired straight away. I'll ring through now on the internal phone. Albert Harrington. That's your man. I hope they won't take too long in tracking him down for you.'

'Thank you very much,' said Sally.

Mr Bainbridge seemed to have now got it into his head that the whole purpose of Sally's visit was to make contact with Albert Harrington, one-time deck steward in the second-class of the SS *Cape St Vincent*. Sally began to think that the elderly clerk really was rather confused in mind, and that the company was indeed keeping him on out of charity. He certainly seemed to know his way about the records put in his charge, however, and about the offices of the Cape and County Line in general. While he was making his enquiries Sally turned back to the passenger lists again. Curtis, she was saying to herself; I wonder if there's anyone called Curtis. The name did not occur at all. But then it was a very long shot, said Sally to herself, and she had not really expected to find it.

She had returned to the copper-plate handwriting of Captain Hudson, and was looking for some clue – she herself really did not know what – among the names of those who had been at his farewell party, when Mr Bainbridge triumphantly produced his information.

'Albert Harrington,' he said, 'transferred to the SS

Huntingdonshire after the *Cape St Vincent* was scrapped, and served on her for three years. He then retired to live in Poplar, and I have noted his address. It is 4 Prospect Terrace. That's on the Isle of Dogs, near the London Docks.'

Mr Bainbridge, looking extremely pleased with himself, produced this information as if this was indeed the climax of Sally's visit, which was now expected to be brought to an end. It seemed to be impossible to return to more general enquiries after this, but as Sally got up from her chair a thought struck her, and she could not resist another question.

'Who was the doctor on the *Cape St Vincent*? I can't see him among Captain Hudson's guests.'

'Doctor? Doctor?' Mr Bainbridge blinked. This change of subject after his triumphant piece of research seemed to disconcert him so much that Sally feared she was going to get no reply, but at last he bent over the captain's diary again and ran his finger down the page, showing signs of annoyance and reluctance for the first time since the beginning of Sally's visit.

'Doctor, doctor.' he muttered. 'Must be somewhere. Surely would have invited the doctor.' He turned the page. 'Here it is.'

It was not surprising that Sally had missed the entry. Captain Hudson had written: 'That completes the list of old friends. Three of those who had only been with me a short while were also present, as follows: Medico (Hall), Assistant Purser (Beveridge), and . . .'

Dr Hall, thought Sally. Who is he and where does he come in?

'There you are then,' said Mr Bainbridge impatiently, and shut up the exercise book.

Sally felt herself dismissed. Perhaps it was time for the old man's lunch break, or perhaps he was suddenly just too tired to talk any more. She longed to ask whether she might borrow Captain Hudson's diary to take away and study at leisure, but knew there was no hope of this. All she could do, after thanking Mr Bainbridge once more for tracking down the deck steward for her, was to venture one last very general question. A combination of nervousness and desperation caused her to put it clumsily.

'Did they ever have any trouble on any of the *Cape St Vincent* voyages – something of a criminal nature, I mean?'

'Trouble! Indeed no.' Mr Bainbridge was very indignant. 'What a very peculiar idea. There is *never* any trouble of such a nature on any of the ships of the Cape County Line.'

Sally gave up, thanked him yet again, and made her goodbyes.

Chapter Ten

THE ALLEYWAY WAS not much lighter than the cavernous offices had been, but when Sally came out into Ludgate Hill the clouds suddenly parted and the great dome of St Paul's stood out clear and solid and comforting against the blue sky.

Sally stood for a moment staring up at it, feeling bewildered and disoriented, as if she had taken a leap out of time and place and was not sure yet where she had landed. Then she walked the few yards up the hill and crossed the road to stand on the lower steps of the cathedral. She had arranged to meet Uncle James here at half past twelve to have lunch with him in the City, and she had been so long in the offices of the Cape and County Line that it was almost that time now. Sally climbed half-way up the steps so as to get a better view of the direction from which she expected Uncle James to come. The roadway was full of traffic, and there were many people on the pavements. Nothing within her line of vision gave the least suggestion that she was standing in the heart of the capital city of a nation – and empire – at war. Her own mind was still hovering uneasily between past and present. The impression of the old clerk talking about the old ship was still strongly with her, and she had to keep reminding herself that the year was now 1939, that her uncle would soon be coming, and that a decision would have to be taken as to what, if anything, she was going to tell him of her researches and the reason for them.

Sally was still gazing down Ludgate Hill, and trying to bring some order into the confusion of her thoughts, when she heard her uncle's voice behind her.

'Not late, am I?'

'Gosh, you gave me quite a fright! I thought you'd be getting off the Number Eleven bus.'

'Decided to come out early,' he replied, 'and keep out of your mother's way. Dropped in to see a man in Paternoster Row.'

'Did you buy anything?' asked Sally. Uncle James collected old books and prints if they had to do with his favourite sports – cricket and boxing – but he seldom talked of his hobby in the family circle because neither Rose nor Mrs Livingstone had any interest in it.

'Nothing worth having. Trade's dead, so he tells me. He's already shifted half his stock to the country for safety's sake.' Uncle James shook his head. 'Doubt if I shall live to see it come back. This war's going to last a long time, and nothing will be the same when it's over.'

'Cheer up, Uncle,' said Sally as they crossed the road. 'There'll be some things that stay the same. We've just passed one of them.' And she tilted her head back over her shoulder in the direction of the great dome, now behind them. 'Built to last.'

'I wonder,' said Uncle James. 'I wonder.'

'Oh, for pity's sake!' cried Sally, beginning to feel rather impatient with her uncle's determined gloom, 'they're not going to bomb St Paul's! What on earth would be the sense of that?'

'Anything could happen,' replied James Davenant as grimly as ever. 'You know, Sal, St Paul's has always stood for London for me. Comes of working in the City, I suppose. You can keep your Westminster Abbey and Buckingham Palace for all I care. As far as I'm concerned that's my London. The dome of St Paul's. That's London for me.'

'And it's going to stay London for you,' said Sally firmly, 'even if you live to be a hundred-and-one. Where are we going to eat?'

'Bullers,' said Uncle James naming an establishment of great age and reputation.

Sally gave a little squeal of excitement. 'That'll be fun.'

She rather changed her attitude, though, when they arrived at the narrow, discreet entrance of the famous eating-place. A tall man in a maroon uniform held open the door for her, and seeing straight ahead an area containing tables laid out with cutlery and white napkins, she automatically took a step towards it. The maroon-clad man, with a movement that succeeded at the same time in being both commanding and deferential, placed himself between her and the tables and bowed slightly.

'Mr Davenant's table reservation is on the first floor, madam,' he said. 'This way, please.'

The first-floor room was panelled in dark oak, and seemed to Sally almost as gloomy as the Cape and County offices. There were very few people eating there, but those few took no notice of them as they entered. When they had ordered their meal she asked her uncle why they were not sitting in the more pleasant room downstairs, and was told that the first floor was the ladies' annexe, the ground floor and the second floor being reserved for gentlemen only. Sally was indignant.

'Honestly, Uncle James, you'd think we were back in the Dark Ages, not nearly half-way through the twentieth century. If this is the sort of thing the war's going to do away with, then I can only say I think it's all to the good. I've a good mind to go down and walk around all those stuffed shirts guzzling away downstairs and say, "Look at me – I'm a human female! I've just as much right to exist as you have, and if it's spoiling your meal to be reminded of my existence that's just too bad!" '

James Davenant looked rather apprehensive, and Sally hastily assured him that she was going to behave correctly. Chris would not approve of a place like this, she suddenly found herself thinking; he's got a quite a different sort of attitude towards women. It was this thought that decided Sally to say nothing to her uncle about her suspicions of Christian. The truth, if she ever discovered it, was a matter for Chris and herself alone, and she would never discuss him with anybody else. Frank was a different matter, and she proceeded to give her uncle a brief account of the incident on the *Cape St Vincent*, adding that she had thought at first that Frank was the man she had seen, but that she was now beginning to think that she had been mistaken in this.

Uncle James looked at first puzzled, then incredulous, then puzzled again.

'But why didn't you tell anybody about it, Sally?' he asked several times. 'You ought to have told your mother and it would have been investigated at once. You weren't an infant. You were eleven years old. You ought to have told somebody straight away.'

'But I did try to!' cried Sally. 'I tried telling the stewardess and the doctor. At least, I suppose he was the doctor. It was somebody she brought along in a white coat, I don't remember noticing anything else about him. I tried to tell them, and they didn't believe me. They thought I was hysterical. And I really was dreadfully sick. Have you ever been seasick, Uncle James? Really bad, I mean. You don't care if you're letting fifty murderers get away with it so long as they leave you alone and let you die in peace.'

Uncle James made some of his little grunting noises and then said: 'How about later on, when you felt better? Why didn't you say something about it then? Give them a chance to investigate before the boat docked at Southampton.'

'I didn't stop being sick until the boat docked at Southampton,' retorted Sally. 'And even then I went and started again in the car. Don't you remember you had to keep stopping when you were driving us back to Oxford?'

James Davenant's face softened, and in a gesture of tenderness rare in him he reached out a hand and gently touched Sally's as it rested on the table, the fingers gripping the stem of her wineglass. 'I remember it well,' he said. 'The first time I ever saw you. Poor little scrap, I said to myself. So pale and thin and weak we nearly had to carry you to the car. But you were very independent, even then. When we got to Weir House you wouldn't have your mother or your Aunt Gertrude help you to bed. Oh no, you could manage all on your own, thank you. And you soon perked up and got the roses back in your cheeks again, and once you began to eat there was no stopping you. But you could have told me about it then, my dear. I really do think you ought to have mentioned it then.'

'I suppose I ought,' said Sally slowly. Her fingers relaxed and she began to eat again. 'But I was full of other things by then. Getting used to life in England, and school, and everything so different. It all seemed so far away and unreal by then. Like a dream, or things you imagine when you're in a fever. I suppose I didn't want to think about it. I suppose I was trying to believe that it had never happened.'

'Sally,' said Uncle James leaning forward and speaking quietly and very seriously, 'do you think that is the answer? Do you think that this never really happened at all, but that you were very feverish and imagined it? Just as the stewardess and the doctor thought?'

'I've wondered that myself,' she replied, 'But I can't seem to rest with that explanation. Ever since I first saw Frank's face and thought it was the same face, I've felt as if I shall never have peace of mind until I know the truth.'

'Even if the truth should turn out to be that no such incident took place and that you've been making yourself miserable without any cause?'

Sally did not immediately reply.

'I think you'd find that hard to take, knowing you,' went on James Davenant. 'Can't say I'd like it myself, discovering I'd been worrying for years over something that never happened. Wouldn't like to feel I'd gone a little bonkers.'

Suddenly Uncle James gave her one of his unexpectedly shrewd glances. 'Is that what's worrying you? Is that why you've taken up with this loony doctor of yours?'

Sally felt herself flushing. 'That's partly why,' she said. 'I do like him for himself, and I like helping in the work he's doing, but I also thought that he might help me get some treatment if I did decide I was having hallucinations and needed sorting out.'

She tried to speak as if she was half laughing at herself, but Uncle James seemed to have no inclination to treat it lightly.

'I don't believe there's anything wrong with you at all,' he said. 'I've always thought you were the most clear-headed girl I've ever known. You've got a bit of a temper, and you tend to exaggerate sometimes, but then all young people do that. But you wouldn't make up stories about anything that really mattered. No. That I don't believe.'

James Davenant shook his head, and then drained his glass as if in defiance.

'I don't believe it either,' said Sally, 'so now we've got that out of the way, please will you help me to prove it was not Frank.'

'Or to prove it was.'

They stared at each other.

'I don't think it would make any difference to Rose,' said Sally at last. 'I thought at first that it might, but I'm afraid she'll stick to him, whatever he's done. It would only make her miserable, that's all.'

I'd stick to Chris, whatever he'd done, Sally added to herself; that's why I know now that Rose will stick to Frank. It feels different if you love somebody.

'If it really happened,' Uncle James was saying, 'that a man pushed a woman out of a porthole on the *Cape St Vincent*, and if that man was the man now calling himself Frank Sedgemore, then the first thing we've got to ask is, does he know that the child who saw him is yourself? Does he know that the Livingstone family was in the next cabin? And if so, has he deliberately sought out the Livingstone family for this very reason?'

Sally had thought of this aspect of the matter, but in her preoccupation with Christian had not given it much attention. 'To check that none of us remembers and that he really is still safe from any enquiry,' she said. 'But if he found out that I did remember and had actually recognized him—'

'Exactly,' said Uncle James.

'Oh, I don't believe it!' cried Sally. 'First of all, I think it's extremely unlikely that it was Frank, but if it was, then I'm sure he doesn't know we were the people in the next cabin. He'd have to be acting a part with us all the time, and I simply don't believe he's as good an actor as all that. Besides, why wait all these years before getting to know us?'

'That stumps me, I admit.' Uncle James thought for a moment. 'Perhaps the meeting with Rose was by chance, and only when he found out who she was did he decide to follow it through. Perhaps he thought she was the child who saw him.'

'So he pretends to fall in love with her and actually gets engaged to her. Because a wife can't give evidence against her husband? Or because he's planning to do away with her too, and will find it easier if they're married? It's no good, Uncle. I just don't believe it.'

'I agree that it is extremely unlikely,' said James Davenant, 'but nevertheless I don't like it.'

'You mean I could be in danger?'

'If your murderer knows you are the one who saw him. Yes.'

The waiter came with their soup. If it was Christian,

130

thought Sally, then I really am in danger whether he cares for me or not. It was strange that she found it difficult to believe that Frank, whom she did not like, was a potential murderer, but easy to believe that Christian, whom she believed she could love, would be capable of anything if he had a strong enough motive. The trouble was that she could not help thinking that his motive would be a good one, whatever the deed itself might be. Could one excuse the taking of a life on the grounds that the motive was good? Sally found that Uncle James had been talking and she had not heard him, but apparently it was only to ask how far she had got with her researches.

She told him of her talk with Mr Bainbridge. 'I think I'll go down to dockland and see the deck steward,' she added. 'He might be able to help, and in any case it would be nice to see him. But I wondered if you could find out yourself whether anything suspicious happened on the *Cape St Vincent*'s last voyage. Whether there was any stowaway. Who was this woman? That's the puzzle. If there'd been a passenger or crew member lost overboard then surely it couldn't have been hushed up. The ship would have been buzzing with gossip. Mother would certainly have been talking about it. But she never said anything, did she?'

James Davenant shook his head. 'Nothing. I never heard of any incident on that voyage at all. Either there was a very big cover-up or else the people concerned were very lucky to get away with it. And since Captain Hudson would never have countenanced any cover-up—'

They were interrupted by the waiter changing the plates. He seemed inclined to linger, and it was some time before Uncle James was able to continue.

'I'll make some tactful enquiries myself,' he said, 'but I doubt if I'll get anything more out of the shipping offices. If there was the slightest hint of scandal, they'd hush it up. In any case, nobody's interested in what happened ten years ago. They are all too much occupied with the present crisis. I should think your deck steward's your best bet, Sally. And the stewardess, if I can track her down for you. And any other of the crew or passengers, but my word, you're going to have your work cut out tracing them all.'

'We'll have to turn ourselves into a private detective agency. Davenant and Livingstone. Doesn't sound right, does it? Sounds more like solicitors or undertakers.'

They both laughed, and were still laughing when the next course arrived. The waiter went away quickly this time, looking rather disappointed.

'Are you going to tell your mother?' asked Uncle James when they were alone again. 'After all, she might be able to help.'

'I'm not very keen to,' said Sally, 'but I suppose we could make a general sort of enquiry, not mentioning Frank, of course. Pushing the stowaway idea, perhaps.'

'Tenerife,' said James Davenant abruptly.

'Yes, I thought it could be someone who had come aboard at Tenerife and stayed there unofficially. That would account for nobody noticing her disappearance.'

'And since it took place in your part of the ship, that's presumably where she was hiding. Were there any empty cabins near you? Or did anybody leave the boat – officially – at Tenerife?'

'That's what I wanted to ask Mr Bainbridge,' said Sally, 'but it was hopeless to go on any longer with him. Gosh, I'd like to be let loose among his records!'

'These are straightforward matters that I might be able to settle without giving the impression that I'm trying to stir up any unpleasantness,' said Uncle James. 'I'll do my best at the Cape and County and let you know.'

'I wonder if you could do something at the Oxford end as well.'

'Oxford? You want me to keep an eye on that fellow's behaviour in Oxford?'

'Well, I don't think it would be a bad idea, but actually what I mean now was to check up on Frank's story of how he got his scar. Was it in a car crash as he says?'

'All right. I'll make enquiries. That ought not to be too difficult.'

'What it is,' cried Sally, 'to have such a tremendously worthy and respected citizen as partner in a detective investigation! Bless you, Uncle James. If Frank did get the scar in that crash then he can't be the man I saw on the boat.'

'That would seem to be so. You're sure about the scar?'

'Absolutely sure. It was very clear and rather frightening. A sort of curved livid mark. Like Frank's.'

'H'm.' Uncle James thought this over. 'I suppose one can fake a scar. These make-up people are deuced clever nowadays. Make you believe anything on a cinema screen.'

'But why should anybody make up their face with a faked scar?'

'Fancy dress party. Or deliberate disguise before carrying out a murder. There's two reasons for you.'

And perfectly good reasons, said Sally to herself, with the great sinking of the heart that now came to her every time her mind tried to face the possibility that it could have been Chris, and for a moment she had an over-whelming impulse to tell her uncle everything and be comforted and guided by him.

There he sat, in his beautifully tailored suit of clerical grey, with his iron-grey hair and bristling moustache, and his blue-grey eyes that saw the world through his own unshakable idea of how things ought to be. It was a rigid and outmoded idea, and in its very lack of imagination it could sometimes be cruel, but it was absolutely honest. James Davenant was as solid and immovable as the dome of St Paul's that meant so much to him. He would stick to the truth, and he would always do his duty, come what may.

It might one day be a very unpleasant duty. Sally knew that he loved his two nieces more than anybody else in the world, and that one of them was already causing him great anxiety. If Frank were shown to have a criminal record and to be breaking the law now, then James Davenant would feel obliged to try to bring him to justice, at whatever cost to his favourite niece Rose. It would be very hard if he should at the same time have to worry because his other niece had fallen in love with a mysteri-ous man who might be a murderer. It was really not fair on Uncle James to tell him all about Chris now.

As they left the restaurant and walked along past the great blank wall of the Bank of England, Sally tried hard to convince herself that this was the reason why she was not fully confiding in her uncle, but she knew it was only a very small part of the truth. The chief reason was that she was afraid for Christian's sake. If he could be proved to be a guilty man, then Uncle James would have no mercy, whereas she herself . . .

How on earth was she going to get it across to Chris that he could entrust her with the truth and that she would keep it to herself for ever?

Chapter Eleven

THE MOMENT SHE SAW Chris again, Sally felt completely sure that he had never committed any offence against humanity, and never would. He was sitting at her desk, typing on the little portable with surprising speed, and standing beside the desk was a middle-aged woman whom Sally took at first to be some sort of social worker.

'I wish you'd let me type it for you, doctor,' she was saying as Sally appeared in the open doorway of the tiny office.

Chris pulled the paper out of the machine. 'There you are,' he said, picking up a pen, 'not perfect, but let's hope it will do the trick. Try that on your boss, Miss Watkins, and if it doesn't work, then come back and we'll think of something else. And if you ever feel like coming to talk about your problem, well, that's what we're here for.'

'It's very kind of you,' said the woman, who, Sally noticed, had a pleasant but rather anxious-looking face, 'but I don't feel I ought to take up your time with such a trivial matter.'

'I don't think it's all that trivial,' said Chris. 'In any case, it would be helpful to us, if you don't mind being used as an anonymous guinea-pig. My colleague and I are making a particular study of phobias in war-time, and the more clinical material for our researches the better. Miss Livingstone will bear me out.'

After Miss Watkins had gone Sally asked Chris what had been the matter with her.

'She works for a solicitor in an office near Euston Station' he replied. 'Apparently he is so worried about air-raids that he's made all the staff crowd into the rooms on the ground floor and he's put Miss Watkins to work in a cubby-hole under the stairs without a window. She suffers badly from claustrophobia and says she can't stand it any longer and would much rather sit upstairs and take her chance, but he won't listen to her, and she doesn't want to give notice because she likes her work and wouldn't find it all that easy to get another job at the moment.'

'So you've written to her boss,' said Sally.

'I've written a sort of certificate, tactfully I hope, and I hope she'll pluck up courage to use it. Good Lord!'

'What is it?'

'She's left us a cheque for five pounds.' Chris handed the slip of paper to Sally. 'She asked if she could make a contribution to our funds, and I expected a shilling or two, as most of them produce.'

'That's two weeks' wages,' said Sally. 'I don't believe she's a solicitor's typist at all. It was only an excuse.'

'Fairy godmother in disguise? Or secret service agent come to check up on us? Anyway, we're in business. I wanted to talk to you about fund-raising in any case. We can't live on Ralph for ever, but there are various legal aspects to be gone into before we start any sort of appeal.'

Sally felt as if her morning's researches and her talk with Uncle James belonged to another world. It was surely quite impossible that murder and sinister mystery could have anything to do with this man who was talking to her so enthusiastically about the work they could achieve if only they had the means. She would drop her enquiries and try to forget the past. Except that she could not drop them now, because she had brought Uncle James in too. And there were other incongruities so great that one could not believe them, and yet one knew them to be true. Her own beloved sister Rose in love with some sort of confidence man, for example. These beautiful autumn days, with the trees in the park golden against the deep blue of the afternoon sky, and at the same time wide-scale death and destruction was not far away. Good and evil, evil and good. They were side by side, inseparable. You only had to turn over the coin. You could not have one without the other. No, it was no use telling herself that Chris as she saw him now was the true, the real, the only Dr Christian Hofmeyr. She must act as if she thought he was, because otherwise their working together would be intolerable, but she must never abandon her search for the truth.

To make the resolution was simple. To carry it out was almost beyond Sally's powers. It was not her nature to play a part and to be a spy, she decided, as Chris dictated the draft of an appeal for funds to run the clinic. Every time he paused for a moment she raised her eyes from her notebook and glanced at him. Did those heavy, slightly tinted spectacles hide a tell-tale mark? Was the skin lighter at the side of the left cheek? Or was it simply due to the way the light and shadow fell?

Perhaps she could arrange a little accident, brush past him in such a way that his glasses would slip or become askew, and then she could see. It would not be difficult in this crowded little office. But the moment she thought of this Sally knew that she could not carry it through. Tricks like that were not in her nature, either. It would be easier for her to say straight out: 'Chris – I suspect you of being the man I saw on the boat. Take off your glasses and let me see the scar.'

Once she believed she came near to doing this, but the telephone rang, and he had a long conversation with what sounded like a woman in great distress at the other end of the line, and when it was over the moment had passed. I will confront him soon, she promised herself as she sat typing a little later, but it must be when we are alone and there's no danger of interruption. When she had finished her work she glanced at her watch. It was past six o'clock, but she had promised to stay on as long as necessary. The house seemed unusually quiet. For some time now there had been no sound of movement, or voices, or of doors opening and shutting.

Sally got up from her desk and looked into the front consulting room. There was nobody there, nor was either Chris or Ralph in any of the other rooms on the ground floor. For a moment she wondered whether they had gone off together on some errand and left her in the place alone. The thought was oddly disturbing; she was not quite sure why. Then it occurred to her that they might have gone upstairs to Ralph's living quarters to talk in greater comfort. She had not heard anybody go upstairs, but then she had been concentrating on her typing. Sally picked up the pile of letters. If they were signed and sent off at once they would catch the post. She heard no sound of voices as she ran upstairs, but when she came on to the

139

first-floor landing she saw that the door of the big room in front was closed, although the bedroom and bathroom doors were open.

Sally hesitated before knocking. She could hear them now: a low murmur, nothing more. Perhaps she had better go back to the office and wait until they came down. After all, this was Ralph's own private residence, as well as a doctor's surgery, and if he chose to ask Chris up for a talk or a drink or anything else she had no right to go barging in. She had just decided not to knock just yet, but to go down and stamp the envelopes and then call loudly up the stairs, when the voices inside the room suddenly became louder and clearer, as if the two men had moved nearer to the door.

'I'm going to have to tell her something.' It was Chris speaking. 'We can't go on like this.'

'What are you going to tell her?' Ralphs' voice was very abrupt.

Christian then spoke again, but this time Sally could not make out the words.

'She's no fool, you know,' said Ralph, 'for all she's such a glamourpuss.'

'I know she's not a fool!'

Christian's voice sounded very loud, and Sally instinctively took a step back away from the closed door. She was eavesdropping, and she could not help herself. She wanted to run away, but her feet refused to move any further.

'Would you like me to speak to her?' she heard Ralph say.

'No!'

The exclamation came with such force from Chris that

140

Sally took another step back. 'You keep your mouth shut,' he went on, 'and if you don't, I'll—'

Sally heard no more. Her legs were loosened, and she ran. In the office she hastily stuck stamps on the envelopes for the letters she had written, scribbled a note to say that she was going now, propped it in the typewriter, put on her hat and coat and hurriedly let herself out of the house.

The moment she had closed the front door behind her she wished she had remained inside. There could surely be no doubt that it was she whom the two doctors had been discussing, but what was it that she was to be told? If only she had stayed another few seconds she might have found out, or at least found out whether it was anything to do with the incident on the *Cape St Vincent*. It could, of course, have been something quite different. Something to do with one or the other of that could affect Sally's attitude towards her work at the clinic. Or it could be to do with Sally herself. Perhaps they had discussed her as a clinical case and had decided that she really was suffering from hallucinations or some sort of mental unbalance. In that case it must be Chris who wanted to consider her feelings, and Ralph who would be less careful of them . . .

Sally stood on the doorstep and looked at the dingy street and raged at herself. She had no key to the house, and could not get in again without ringing the bell. She had had the most wonderful chance to learn something at last, and she had thrown it away. What sort of seeker after truth was that? Or had her flight been due not to cowardice but to her own deep revulsion at being an eavesdropper?

She drew a deep breath, and swore to herself that if ever she had another chance like that she would not let it pass by. All personal feelings had to be set aside, all fears

141

suppressed, all codes of behaviour broken. This was a resolution that she was going to keep if it killed her. Perhaps it would kill her. There were three men now whose lives and actions she was determined to uncover. Two of them – Ralph Curtis and Frank Sedgemore – she was convinced were unscrupulous, and she disliked them both. The third man was different. She believed she could love him, and she could not bear to believe ill of him. She was sure he would not try to destroy her in order to protect himself, but if she discovered that he was indeed an evil man, then she herself would lose all wish to live. And so she was in danger from him too. But neither danger nor disillusionment was going to hold her back. Neither of them were as bad as the torments of doubt. 'From now on there is to be no running away,' she said aloud to herself as she went slowly down the steps.

Ralph's car stood by the kerb. It was what Frank Sedgemore would call a sporty little number, bright red, looking as if it was raring to go. Sally glanced at it, her thoughts momentarily diverted. It would be nice to run about in just such a little car. What a feeling of freedom and adventure it would give.

'Can you drive?' said a man's voice.

Dr Curtis had come out of the house and was standing on the doorstep.

'No. I wish I could,' said Sally.

'I'll teach you if you like. How about your first lesson now?'

Sally's first instinct was to refuse, because there were few things that appealed to her less than driving anywhere with Ralph, but she remembered in time her resolution of a few seconds ago, 'no more running away,' and said instead that it was very kind of him, but that she had promised to be home by seven.

'I'll drive you home, then,' he said, 'and we'll practise a little in the park on the way. That sounds bad, doesn't it,' he added as he opened the door of the passenger seat. 'It's not only driving that one practises in the park.'

Sally ignored this. She would have to put up with Ralph to serve her own ends, but it didn't mean that she need play the sort of girl he wanted her to.

'What about Chris?' she asked as they drove away.

'What about him?'

'Oughtn't we to give him a lift?'

'No. He's staying on late. The woman who phoned in a suicidal condition is coming in. He's going to try to get her into hospital, but it won't be easy. Damned imbeciles!' Ralph took a corner at a terrifying speed, and Sally thought he was referring to the two cyclists who only just managed to get out of his way, but when he went on it was plain that he was actually talking about the civil defence authorities. 'Keeping thousands of hospital beds empty for non-existent air-raid casualties and refusing to admit people who are seriously ill.'

Sally could tolerate Ralph when he talked like this, and the actual driving lesson was not too bad. He showed her the controls, and she sat at the wheel for a few minutes, crawling round the road that encircled Queen Mary's Gardens, and quickly getting the feel of the steering and the brakes.

'You'll soon get the hang of it,' he said as they changed seats. 'Take you out again if you can bear my company.'

Sally could not find anything to say to this. She had not realized quite how much she had allowed her feelings about him to show. He drove on in silence for a few minutes and then pulled up at a spot from which they could see the Mappin Terraces in the Zoo.

'You've got another fifteen minutes,' he said. 'Let's talk for a bit.'

'Suits me,' said Sally.

He turned towards her with all the charm turned on, but all he said was: 'They had quite a problem there – lots of dangerous beasts and the possibility of air-raids.'

'I'd been wondering about that,' said Sally. 'One doesn't like the thought of lions on the loose in addition to everything else.'

'You've no need to worry about that,' said Ralph with a knowing air that reminded Sally fleetingly of Frank. 'They've taken quite sensible precautions, in my humble opinion. The poisonous snakes and spiders have been destroyed, and the keepers are armed and have instructions to shoot instantly if buildings are damaged and animals escape.'

'What a shame!' cried Sally. 'To think of those lovely wild creatures having to be destroyed through no fault of their own.'

She turned to look at him as she spoke, and their eyes met briefly, and then Ralph's slid away. It seemed to Sally that the mask of practised charmer had slipped in that moment, and what she had seen beneath was a worried, perhaps even a frightened, man.

'It won't be only lions and tigers that are destroyed through no fault of their own,' he said recovering himself. 'Not if this war really gets going.'

'D'you think it really will?' asked Sally.

For a short while they discussed the news of the day.

144

We all talk and talk about it, thought Sally, and everyone has an opinion and asks everybody else's opinion, but none of us really knows anything, from the Government downwards nobody really knows anything at all. And it'sprobably just the same with the Germans. We're all helpless puppets. But who's pulling the strings? It can't be God. It must be the Devil. Hitler? But perhaps he's a puppet too.

'I suppose it's all just conjecture,' she said in reply to a remark of Ralph's, and after that there was a short silence. Anyway, he hasn't brought me here to talk about the war, Sally added to herself; we got on to it by mistake and then got stuck. What he really wants is to tell me something about Chris; something connected with that conversation I overheard.

When Ralph next spoke it was as if he had read her thoughts. 'Bit of a slave-driver, isn't he, old Chris,' he said. 'Don't suppose you realized what you were letting yourself in for when you took on the job.'

'I like to work hard,' said Sally. 'Don't you?'

'Me?' He seemed a little taken aback. 'Of course I do. Are you trying to tell me that you don't think I'm pulling my weight?'

This remark was calculated to make Sally feel she was being unfair, and to give Ralph Curtis the advantage. He laughed away her denials and then added, 'Seriously, though, what d'you think of Chris?'

'I like and admire him,' said Sally instantly.

'H'm. Yes. I think there is a distinct resemblance,' said Ralph after taking a long look at her.

Sally shrugged. 'All right. Go ahead. You want to tell me something and I've no objection to hearing whatever it is.'

Ralph made a grimace. 'There's no need to labour the

145

point. I'm not totally dim-witted. You've made it perfectly plain that you don't like me personally, and I promise you that you will not be subjected to unwelcome advances from me. Perhaps I might be promised a bare minimum of courtesy in return.'

Again Sally felt obliged to apologize, feeling that she had behaved with childish rudeness, and disliking him more every moment as she stumbled over the words.

'The resemblance,' said Ralph releasing her from her embarrassment at last, 'is to Chris's wife. A blue-eyed suntanned blonde. Don't look like that. I'm not paying compliments. I'm simply stating facts. Her name was Louise. She treated him abominably from the first, and eventually did him the kindness of running off with somebody else. He didn't think it was a kindness, of course, poor chap. He was absolutely besotted.'

'What became of her?' asked Sally swallowing her own pride and her reluctance to talk about Chris, and reminding herself of her resolution to discover everything she could. Of course, I can't trust him, she added to herself, but even if he's lying it ought to give me some clue.

'I don't think that particular man lasted very long either,' replied Ralph, 'but I can honestly say that I do not know where Louise is at this moment.'

This rather odd way of putting it brought a wild idea to Sally's mind. The woman who drowned at sea. Could it possibly have been the wife whom Chris had loved and who had betrayed him? And did Ralph know about it, and was that the reason why the two men stuck together, not as friends and colleagues, but blackmailer and victim? Except that it was Ralph who had the money,

146

not Chris. And it was Chris, not Ralph, whom Sally had overheard to say that she must be told something.

'I'd like to know what happened to her,' continued Ralph before Sally had had a chance to apply any kind of reason to her racing thoughts. 'She was a bit of a bitch, I admit, but after all, she was my sister.'

'Your sister?' Sally looked at him as she spoke. Yes, that could be true. She found it disagreeable to think that there was any physical similarity between herself and the man sitting beside her, but had to admit that the colouring and build were alike. She could, she supposed, bear a resemblance to the sister of this man. 'Does Chris think I look like Louise?' she added.

'Very much so. The likeness is quite striking. We've both remarked on it.'

Sally felt hurt and annoyed with herself for being hurt. Even if Chris had taken to her in the first place because she reminded him of the wife he'd loved, surely that didn't mean that since then he hadn't come to value her for herself. Indeed, she had ample evidence that he had.

'You've really fallen for him, haven't you?' went on Ralph, looking at her closely.

'If you're determined to think so, then there's no point in my contradicting you,' said Sally.

'I'm sorry for you,' he said after looking steadily at her for a little longer.

'Am I supposed to ask why?'

Again he took some time to reply. At last he said: 'You don't really know anything about Chris, do you?'

'What does any one of us really know about another?' she countered.

'Precious little,' he admitted. 'Even those of us who

have studied psychology. But there are certain things in a person's life that can be stated as facts. Date of birth, for example. Whether married or single. Whether ever served a prison sentence or committed an indictable offence. These are the sort of things about which it is possible to be sure.'

'It would seem so,' agreed Sally, feeling quite sure now that it was Ralph's aim to discredit Christian in her eyes. No doubt he was determined to get his story in first after Chris had said that Sally would 'have to be told something', but she suspected that there was also an element of hurt vanity in Ralph's remarks about Chris.

'My sister was very much sought after,' he said. 'Our parents were very disappointed when she chose Chris. Not that there was anything particularly wrong with him. He'd qualified, and had a job to go to, and he'd even got a little bit of capital of his own, but all the same, to go and choose the son of a Boer farmer, when there were several very eligible Englishmen after her . . . she was presented at court, you know, and was a great success in the London season. It did seem a bit of a come-down, and I can quite understand how my parents felt.'

Sally took a grip on herself before speaking. If she was not very careful she was going to flare up as she had done with her mother, and no purpose would be served in having a row with Ralph Curtis.

'I don't think my father would have shared their feelings,' she said as calmly as she could. 'He'd have said we were all just South Africans, English and Afrikaner and Malay and Hottentot alike.'

'Really?' Dr Curtis raised his eyebrows. 'A rather unusual attitude, if I may say so. What was his line during

148

the flag controversy? Would he have had the Union Jack left out altogether?'

'If it made for national unity, yes,' said Sally defiantly.

'All very idealistic, I'm sure,' said Ralph with something like a sneer. 'I'm afraid my folks were much more prejudiced. I had a cousin who even went so far as to summon the children round the table and make them kiss the Union Jack and swear that they'd always be true to the home country and never give in. Somewhat melodramatic and exaggerated, but it gives you the idea of how my people felt when Louise married Chris.'

'She would have been a faithful wife to an eligible Englishman, no doubt,' said Sally coolly.

Ralph laughed and addressed an invisible audience. 'The girl's got a bite. She's not just a pretty face! No,' he added, 'I'm sorry to say I don't think Louise would have been much of a wife to any man. She was far too spoilt. All I'm trying to say is that the marriage with Chris was even more likely to be unsuccessful then the other possible marriages. He wouldn't see that, of course. He worshipped her. Hadn't a notion what she was really like. When he found out he went berserk. Swore he'd murder her. Did a most convincing Othello act.'

Ralph paused, but Sally said nothing.

'It's more than ten years ago now,' he went on, 'that she ran off with this American, and we never heard any more. My parents died not knowing. I wonder if I shall ever find out what did become of her.'

Sally gripped her hands together. I am not going to comment, she said to herself; I am not going to ask anything.

'Of course,' he said, 'she may have lain low because she

149

was afraid of Chris. Don't get me wrong, Sally. He's my oldest friend, and he's a first-class man at his job, but he's got a temper and he takes things to heart. You want to be careful with Chris. You don't want to get on the wrong side of him. I thought it only fair to warn you.'

'I'm not getting you wrong,' said Sally even more coldly than before. 'I believe I understand you very well.'

'Do you?' He suddenly produced the charming smile. 'Well, if you do, it's more than I do myself. We'd better move on. Your folks will be sending out a search party.'

'Tell me,' said Sally just before they drew up at Park Mansions, 'you've been backwards and forwards to Cape Town quite a lot. Did you ever travel on the *Cape St Vincent*?'

'I was on one of those old tubs once,' replied Ralph. 'Was it the *St Vincent*? Or was it one of the other Cape boats?' He appeared to think for a moment. 'Sorry,' he said at last. 'Can't remember which one it was. Does it matter?'

'Not really,' said Sally getting out of the car. 'I just wondered. Thanks for the lift. Excuse me not inviting you in, but there's packing up for a move going on, and I don't think it will be very comfortable.'

'That's all right,' he said. 'I'll look forward to meeting your sister another time.'

He drove away, and as Sally pushed open the main door of the block she tried to remember whether she had mentioned to Ralph Curtis that she had a sister. At the door of No. 3 she decided that she had not said anything about Rose, which meant that Chris must have told him. There was nothing very surprising in that, but nevertheless it made Sally feel all the more uneasy. What Ralph had just told her might or might not be true. On the whole she was inclined to think that Chris really had married his sister, but whatever lay behind the rest of the tale, she had no doubt at all that Ralph was deliberately hinting that Chris might have done some harm to Louise. Which could only mean that Chris had told him Sally's own story.

I suppose I am to believe that it was Chris whom I saw, and that the woman he was pushing through the porthole was Louise, said Sally to herself as she turned the key in the lock. Now why should it be to the interest of Dr Curtis that I should suspect Christian? Sally could not even begin to guess at a reason. All she knew when she came into the hall of the flat was that her vague dislike of Ralph had turned into a loathing and distrust of him so deep that in comparison with it she thought of her mother with tolerance and goodwill, if not affection.

Chapter Twelve

SARAH LIVINGSTONE GREETED Sally with something approaching warmth. Perhaps she sensed the rare but genuine goodwill in her younger daughter, or perhaps it was simply because her resentment was temporarily diverted to the elder, since Rose and Frank were apparently out and not likely to be back until late.

'Never mind,' said Sally soothingly. 'You go and have a rest now, and I'll cook the dinner, and we'll have a quiet evening, you and Uncle James and me.'

It turned out to be a very peaceful evening, for which Sally was grateful after all her wildly changing moods of the day. Sarah Livingstone did not even need to be amused by card games, but was content to listen to the wireless for a little and then talk to her brother. He was in a nostalgic mood, recalling incidents of their childhood at Weir House. Sally soon drifted off into her own thoughts, but after a while something he said brought her mind into full attention again.

'Do you remember, Sarah, arriving at Southampton with the girls on that bitterly cold day? I felt so sorry for you all.'

Sarah Livingstone gave a little shudder. 'Oh, my dear, it was absolutely frightful! What a voyage! Sally was sick all the way and Rose was at that awkward age when people didn't know whether to treat her as a child or as a grown-up, and the stewards were so rude and unobliging . . . never again, never, never again do I travel second-class on a Cape and County boat. Or on any other boat, for that matter. I've never particularly liked travelling in any case, and to be in such discomfort . . .'

Mrs Livingstone gave another little shudder, accompanied by a grimace of disgust.

'It was awfully squashed, wasn't it,' said Sally, suddenly realizing that there was a purpose behind her uncle's apparently random remark. 'I know I felt very shut in, down on that lower deck, and I was always longing to be well enough to get upstairs and into the air. And yet I don't remember seeing many other people from the cabins near to us. Were there people in the next cabin or the one opposite, Mother? Do you remember?'

Sally found it difficult to make this sound like a casual enquiry, and was relieved when her mother answered with no suspicion of any deeper motive. 'There was that perfectly frightful couple next door, not the sort of people one expects to have to associate with. They were dirty, James. Really dirty. And to have to use the same bathroom! In any case, I never feel that salt water coming through the taps can be really clean. The woman tried to scrape acquaintance with me once. I do remember that. But I soon settled it, and she never tried again. Extraordinary, isn't it,' added Sally's mother. 'You forget all about these things for years, and then suddenly it comes back to you. I can see that woman's face as clearly as if it was yesterday. Badly dyed hair, and rouge laid on with a trowel, and a common accent. Most extraordinary.'

153

It is indeed most extraordinary, thought Sally, how you remember a face. Or think you do. But the woman whom her mother had mentioned could not possibly be the woman pushed through the porthole, because she had mentioned a couple. Unless . . .

'What was the husband like?' she asked. 'I don't remember ever seeing either of them.'

'Husband?' Sally's mother made a little gesture of contempt. 'Oh – insignificant, I suppose. I don't really remember.'

'Then he can't have been that tall dark man I once saw,' said Sally.

'Where?' demanded her mother, looking at her daughter with eyes so alert that Sally wished she had not said this.

'I can't really remember,' she said. 'Coming from the bottom of the stairs, I think. You were all up in the dining saloon, and I wanted to go into the bathroom, but as soon as I opened the cabin door I saw a man in the corridor so I went back into the cabin.'

'You probably imagined it,' said her mother. 'There wasn't any tall dark man in our part of the ship. Two single ladies, I seem to remember, besides that awful couple. I believe the cabin opposite was empty. In fact, there was nobody on that voyage worth talking to at all, not even in the first-class lounge. The dreariest collection of people imaginable . . . and the rudeness of that stewardess! How on earth she expected me to stop you from being sick, Sally, I really don't know. Everybody knows there is nothing on earth you can do about seasickness. Nelson was seasick. It's just one of those things.'

The rude stewardess, thought Sally, and suddenly she

knew, by intuition or by buried memory, what the rudeness had consisted in. The stewardess had thought that Mrs Livingstone was not warm and sympathetic enough towards the sick child, and had had the presumption to tell her so. So this was another little piece of the puzzle slipped into place. Only a background piece: the main picture was still a long way from becoming clear.

'I was much better this last trip,' said Sally. 'Perhaps it is something that you grow out of eventually.'

'Didn't the doctor help at all?' asked James Davenant of his sister.

Sally glanced at him. He sounded only mildly interested, just as she hoped she had sounded herself, but she knew that he had engineered this conversation and was determined to persist with it. Uncle James had taken matters into his own hands, and for a moment she almost wished she had not confided in him at all.

'Doctors!' exclaimed Sarah Livingstone contemptuously. 'I've no faith in doctors. Especially ship's doctors. They only do the job because they've made such a hash of their profession on shore that nobody else will have them.'

Sally was used to her mother's extreme and often unpredictable expressions of opinion, but this one rather surprised her. Later she discovered that her mother had recently been to a lecture that had set her toying with the idea of becoming a Christian Scientist.

'Do you remember the doctor on the *Cape St Vincent*?' she asked, feeling that she was treading on dangerous ground, and that Uncle James had pushed her there.

'An odiously conceited young man,' said Mrs Livingstone. 'Yes, I do remember him. Flirted with the stewardesses and even tried ogling Rose. At her age! She was only a child, and I told him so.'

'Rose never told me,' said Sally, feeling that the gap between herself and her sister was growing ever wider, but also feeling that another little piece of the jigsaw had slipped into place. 'He came to see me once,' she added. 'When the fancy dress party was on. I felt so bad that I rang for the stewardess and she brought the doctor, but I can't remember anything about him except that he wore a white coat, and I don't believe they did anything for me at all.'

'I'm quite sure they didn't, said Mrs Livingstone tartly. 'Probably made you worse, if anything. You were sicker than ever for the rest of the journey.'

Sally felt unable to respond to this, or indeed to take the conversation any further, and she was grateful when her uncle let it drop too. When the wireless was turned on for the news that had already been read several times that day, Sally withdrew into her own thoughts again. It had been salutary, she decided, to hear her mother's recollections of the *Cape St Vincent* voyage. Mrs Livingstone's straightforward self-centredness had brought her daughter some release from the nightmarish insubstantiality of her own memories. It had also shown that their part of the ship had not been fully occupied, and that there had been at least one empty cabin that might have sheltered a stowaway.

Here was one positive gain from the conversation. The other gain was a negative one. Listening to her mother talk, Sally had felt it to be less, rather than more likely that Frank Sedgemore was the man she was seeking. If he had been on that boat then the odds were that Sally's mother would have seen him. She took far more notice of other people's appearance than Sally ever did, and had a good memory for faces. The remark she had let fall about all the passengers being dreary, even in the first-class lounge, showed that she had in fact found her way there, probably a number of times during the three-week voyage. If Frank had been on that boat and Sally's mother had talked to him even for a short while, then she would have remembered him when he came into her life again, and would have made no secret of it.

Or would she? Could one take anything for granted at all? Rose had certainly changed. Or perhaps she had always been like that and Sally had not realized it. Perhaps their mother was not what she had always seemed to be. Perhaps she was, after all, capable of keeping a secret. She had looked surprisingly alert when Sally had mentioned seeing a tall dark man in their part of the ship. Suppose Frank had been on board and Sarah Livingstone had seen him and had later recognized him, but was keeping quiet about it for some reason of her own. What sort of reason could it be?

Sally's mind began to lurch about like a ship in rough seas. She could think of reasons, of course, but not the sort of reasons that one would ever want to connect with one's own mother, however unmotherly she had always been to oneself.

Sally looked across at the two older people, who were sitting side by side on the settee. Neither of them seemed to be attending to the voice of the newsreader. James Davenant was resting his head on his hand and staring at the carpet, and Sarah Livingstone was leaning back against the cushions with her eyes closed, and her face sagging a little as if she were asleep. She looked tired and aging, and Sally felt a rare little stirring of pity, combined with the conviction that whatever involvement she might have with Frank, it was a comparatively venial one. Turning a blind eye to black market operations, yes; anything like the sort of ideas that had been going through Sally's mind, definitely no.

Mrs Livingstone yawned, got up, and left the room, and Sally and her uncle talked as they made up the bed for him on the large settee.

'I've been telephoning about Frank's accident,' he said, 'and had a stroke of luck. The hospital they took him to was a little cottage hospital near Didcot, and the matron remembers him well. I think we can take it that he got the scar six years later than the voyage in question.'

'But if the man I saw had used a scar as a disguise, as you suggested yourself,' said Sally, 'then it could still have been Frank.'

'H'm. That's stretching coincidence a bit far.'

'It's a coincidence that the man I saw should have a scar like Frank's, and yet it happened,' retorted Sally.

'H'm,' said Uncle James again. 'I think perhaps it would be better if we try to put aside what you think you remember and stick to the facts we know. The facts we know about Frank are that he has a history of shady financial dealings, as I found out when I made enquiries after Rose said she wanted to marry him, but that so far nothing can actually be proved against him. Nor do we know where he was at the time of the voyage, but we will find out. Now, as regards the voyage, your mother confirms that there were empty cabins. She denies seeing anybody in your part of the boat resembling the man you describe, and I don't think we had better press her any

158

further, but you might make tactful enquiries of Rose.'

'I certainly shall!' cried Sally.

'Careful, now. Don't go making accusations against Frank. Just keep it general, as we did this evening. Meanwhile I'll get on to Bob Baines again about the stewardess and other possibilities, and when I come up to town again for a day next week we'll go and look up this deck steward together. And, Sally.'

Sally paused at the door of the room. For once she was anxious to get away from Uncle James. The honesty of those blue-grey eyes was beginning to unnerve her.

'I'm doing my best to help you clear up this business that is obviously worrying you so much, but I don't think it's fair of you to hamper me by keeping things back. Are you keeping back any information or even any suspicions that could be of use?'

Sally shook her head. 'Nothing,' she said. 'I don't know anything other than what I've told you.'

She was amazed how genuine it sounded. I don't know myself either, she thought; I always believed I was incapable of an outright lie.

'Let me know if you make any progress,' said Uncle James. Was there a slight reserve or even some disappointment in his voice? Sally could not be sure. 'And do take care, Sal,' he went on. 'We don't know yet whether or nor you're uncovering a murder, but you're certainly digging into things that some people would rather have left alone. Don't take any risks. I beg you, for all our sakes.'

'I'll be very careful,' said Sally, coming across to kiss him good night, and knowing perfectly well that if she saw a chance of getting at the truth she was not going to be careful at all.

Chapter Thirteen

'ISN'T IT WONDERFUL,' said Rose, doing a pirouette in the hall, 'to be rid of them and have the place to ourselves.'

Sally agreed, but in fact she had been sorry to see her mother and uncle go, and the flat felt very empty without them.

'What we'll do,' continued Rose, without paying much attention to her, 'is have a foursome at-home. I'm sick to death of having to go out in the blackout to get away from the family. I'll do the cooking, and Frank will bring the wine, and you must ring up your doctor friend, and we'll have a lovely evening.'

'I think he's gone away for the weekend,' said Sally.

This was not true. She had no idea where Chris was or what he was doing, and she had actually been rather hoping that he might telephone to invite her out. Was he avoiding her because he knew that such a *tête-à-tête* would result in a confrontation? Or was it Ralph's doing? Whatever the reason for it, Sally could not help feeling disappointed and even hurt, and Rose's attitude was increasing that hurt.

'Can't you ring him and see?' asked Rose.

'There's no point if he's away,' said Sally. 'Anyway, I don't feel I know him well enough to invite him to dinner at home.'

Rose made a little pout, a sign that she was annoyed at not getting her own way, and suggested that Sally should ring Charles Brent instead.

'He's in Scotland,' said Sally. 'I phoned last night and the housekeeper said they wouldn't be back for another week.'

'Well isn't there anybody else you can think of?' said Rose impatiently.

'Nobody I want to ask,' said Sally. 'Can't the three of us have a meal together? I've no objection to being man-less, and you never used to mind about such things.'

Rose made a face again.

'I'll stay in my room after dinner if you and Frank want a snogging session,' continued Sally. 'You don't need to worry about me.'

'There's no need to be sarcastic,' said her sister. 'You know I don't mean anything of the sort. I just thought it would be fun to have a bit of a party for a change, and you seemed so keen on this doctor of yours.'

'He's not this doctor of mine,' snapped Sally, 'and we're seeing plenty of each other at work.'

'Oh, I see. Quarrelled already. I suppose you've been holding forth with your opinions, and he didn't like it. Men don't like it, you know.'

'Oh for heaven's sake!' cried Sally. 'You sound like Mother giving her lecture on how to find a husband!'

'You're jealous. That's what it is. You're jealous.'

They were shouting now, both of them, standing just inside the sitting-room door, glaring at each other, two sisters who up till this moment had had only the mildest of tiffs over unimportant matters, both tall and blue-eyed and fair, the elder with the more perfect features, the younger with an air of restless energy about her that the other lacked.

'You haven't given Frank a chance,' stormed Rose. 'You took a dislike to him the moment you saw him and you've been sneering at him ever since. Just because he hasn't got a posh accent and has had to fight for his living!'

'I've not been sneering at him!'

'Oh yes, you have. Don't think I haven't noticed. He's very sensitive about these things. You've got a way of looking at people when you don't think they're up to the mark, and it's sheer hypocrisy, pretending to care so much about social justice and turning your nose up at Frank. You're an even worse snob than Mother, for all your fine words!'

Sally was horrified at the violence of her own anger with her sister. It had been building up, she realized, ever since she got home. She scarcely knew why she felt so angry. All she knew was that Rose seemed to have changed, and it was not for the better. The taunt of jealousy was bad enough, but it had just enough truth in it to silence Sally for a moment. Jealous of Rose's engagement she certainly was not, but there were moments when she envied Rose her more placid and pliable nature, and other moments when she could not help but feel hurt by their mother's clear preference for her sister. So, even in her present fury, Sally could just admit the justice of an accusation of jealousy. But to be called a snob and a hypocrite was so monstrously unfair that all discretion, common sense, and self-control temporarily deserted her.

'I don't dislike Frank because of his origins!' she yelled. 'That's the best part of him. He's worked for himself. But it's what he does that I don't like. I don't think he's straight.'

'What do you mean by that!' Rose took a step nearer to Sally. Her voice had dropped as Sally's grew even louder, but there was something watchful and threatening in her attitude, like a cat about to pounce.

'I don't believe in the office agency', cried Sally beginning to regret her outburst but too carried away to be able to stop herself, 'and neither does Uncle James.'

'Uncle James,' repeated Rose still very softly. 'I see. So you've been trying to turn Uncle against Frank.'

'I've not been trying anything. He can't stand Frank. He told me so the moment I got home. He thinks he's a war profiteer.'

'Then why doesn't he tell me outright if that's what he thinks? I don't believe he said so. You're making it up.'

'I am not making it up!' shouted Sally. 'Uncle James hasn't told you because he doesn't want to upset you. But he's worried to death. And anyhow, it isn't only that. Frank may well be a murderer.'

'A murderer!' Rose's voice was suddenly shrill again, but she quickly brought it under control. 'Just what do you mean by that? Would you care to explain?'

Sally had taken a step backwards, and was leaning against the side of the settee, pressing her hands to her mouth, appalled at what she had said.

'I'm waiting,' said Rose.

Sally let her hands drop. 'I'm sorry,' she muttered. 'I didn't mean it. Silly mistake. Let's try to forget it.'

'You have just said that the man whom I intend to marry may be a murderer. I think I deserve an explanation.'

'It's all a mistake. I'm sure it must be a mistake.'

Sally sank down on to the settee and held a hand over her eyes. Her head felt as if it was bursting and she would have given anything to undo the last few minutes.

'What is a mistake?' asked Rose. 'Why did you say that Frank might be a murderer? I'm going to marry him, so I've got a right to know. Haven't I got a right to know?'

We are not so unlike after all, thought Sally hopelessly. Once we get hold of something we can't let it go. Neither of us. I jump in at the deep end; Rose wades in slowly; but neither of us ever gives up. Whatever it costs, we both go on to the bitter end.

'Yes, you've got a right to know,' she said aloud. 'I ought to have told you straight away. You remember coming to England for the first time on the *Cape St Vincent*?'

'Of course I remember,' said Rose. She perched on the arm of a chair, facing Sally. The tension in her relaxed slightly, but she still looked very wary and very hostile as she listened to Sally's story.

Sally told it as quickly as she could. 'I tried to tell the stewardess and the doctor,' she concluded, 'but they weren't much help.'

'They wouldn't be,' said Rose contemptuously. 'The stewardess was a silly old fusspot, and the doctor was always chasing the girls. He probably pushed the body through the porthole himself.'

'Do you remember him?' asked Sally eagerly. 'Can you remember what he looked like? I can't remember at all.'

Rose considered for a moment. At least she believes me, thought Sally; at least she doesn't blame me for not telling Mother or anybody else. Enemies they might be hence-

164

forth, but they were enemies who understood each other, who had no need to explain or excuse.

'He was quite good-looking,' said Rose at last, 'and he knew it. I can't stand that type.'

'But what did he look like? Was he tall? Lanky? Dark-haired and dark-skinned?'

Rose shook her head. 'Not particularly tall, as far as I can remember. Just average. And certainly not dark. Fair hair. Or light brown. I can't remember. Not particularly thin either. Just ordinary.'

'Then he can't have been the man I saw.' Sally's brief hope was dashed. Even this terrible quarrel with her sister would have been worth while if only it had led to a solution of her mystery. But it seemed to have left her as far away as ever. 'You never saw anyone like that in our part of the boat?' she asked.

Rose shook her head. 'Can't remember anybody.'

'How about in the first-class lounge?' It had suddenly occurred to Sally that if the R. C. Hofmeyr in the passenger list was indeed Christian, then surely he must have sometimes sat in the first-class lounge. 'Did you ever go over there with Mother?' she asked.

'Yes. Now and then. I didn't really want to. I was afraid we'd be found out and get into trouble, but Mother dragged me over. There were some terribly boring old women talking about their ailments, and an American family with some frightfully rude children. I can't remember anyone the least bit interesting. Certainly no unattached young man.'

'So you never saw anybody who could have been the man I saw?'

Rose shook her head again. But if it was Chris on the

boat, thought Sally, then he wouldn't go and sit in the lounge; he'd hate the sort of conversations going on there; he'd stay out on deck, or in the writing-room.

'What about the fancy dress party?' she asked, very unwilling to let go her questioning of Rose without having discovered some little clue. 'Did you see any tall thin dark man there?'

'I don't remember anybody in particular,' said Rose impatiently. 'When are we going to get to Frank?'

'Now,' replied Sally. 'You see, the man I saw in the bathroom had a scar under the left eye. It was not very big, but it showed up very clearly. It was in the same place as Frank's scar. When I first saw Frank the night I got home I knew his face at once. Or rather I believed I did.'

'I see,' said Rose. She was still sitting on the arm of the chair. Her arms were folded and she looked at Sally broodingly. 'I see,' she said again. For a moment or two she remained silent and then she unfolded her arms, stood up, and said briskly: 'It's a mistake, of course. Just as you said. Frank got the scar from a car crash five years ago. And I believe he was in America that winter when we first came to England. It's a pity you didn't tell me about this straight away so that I could have put your mind at rest at once instead of brooding over it all these days.'

'What are you going to do?' asked Sally.

She had got up from the settee and moved towards the door of the sitting-room. They faced each other again, both quite calm now, but even more estranged than during the moments of fury.

'Do?' echoed Rose. 'Need you ask? I'm going to tell Frank straight away, of course. It'll be up to him to decide what to do to free himself from this ridiculous accusation. He may decide just to laugh it off as not worth bothering about. Or he may feel that he has to take it further, since Uncle James has been dragged in too, and his reputation is at stake. I shan't try to influence him.' Rose was in the hall, putting on her hat in front of the mirror as she spoke. 'I'm going to meet him at the office now.' She picked up her bag. 'If there's anything else you'd like me to tell him, then now's your chance.'

Presumably this was an invitation to apologize, but Sally was speechless. Anger, distress, and apprehension combined to make her incapable of any reaction.

'I'm still amazed that you didn't say something at once,' was Rose's parting shot, 'since you always burst out with things. I suppose you were frightened of Frank.' She made her little pout once more. 'And I always used to think you'd got courage, at any rate.'

The front door closed behind her. Sally returned to the settee in the sitting-room. After a little while the tears began to force themselves out painfully, and then at last flowed freely. Fears and doubts and suspicions all faded away. Both Christian and Frank were as if they had never been. Even the wail of the air-raid siren could not rouse her out of the grief that alone remained of the turmoil of emotions. She wept uncontrollably, mourning the loss of her first and nearest love, the sister and companion with whom she had shared all the earliest experiences of life, and with whom she knew there could never be true friendship again.

When the all-clear sounded Sally got up and went to the bathroom and splashed cold water over her face. Then she looked at her watch. It was half past one. If Rose had really gone to the office to meet Frank she would be there by now. Presumably they would have lunch together, and Rose would tell him then that Sally had suspected him of being a murderer. How would he react? Well, that depended, of course, on whether or not he was guilty. If he was not guilty, then surely he would be anxious to take steps to prove it. And if he could prove it, then at least something would have been gained. She would be that much further in finding a solution to the mystery. But if after all he were guilty . . .

Don't accuse people of murder, Uncle James had said, and do take care. It was just as well that he knew nothing about this, thought Sally, and by the time he learnt what she had done whatever was going to happen would already be over. For a moment she felt a little chill of panic, and then her reason reasserted itself. What, after all, had she got in the way of evidence against Frank? Nothing, as her uncle had pointed out, except her own recognition of him. And, as Chris had pointed out, that was very unreliable. On that evidence alone Frank was certainly not going to take the risk of making away with her to keep her quiet. Especially when she had told both Rose and Uncle James of her suspicions, and, for all Frank knew, other people as well. He could hardly murder the lot of them; he would bluff it out.

It might be as well to get it over quickly, this first meeting with them after Rose had told her story. Sally found the number of Frank's office, rang it, and waited for some minutes before reluctantly deciding that there was nobody there. The urge to action was upon her again. She would have liked to have the showdown with Frank, but since this would have to wait she would have to get on with the other line of enquiry: Christian himself. Should she tackle him straight away, or should she first of all follow up her other clue – the deck steward? Albert Harrington, 4 Prospect Terrace, Poplar in East London. Perhaps it would be best to go and see Albert Harrington and try to obtain a few definite facts from an unbiased observer that could help to dispel some of this fog of suspicion.

She studied the London guide to find out exactly where he lived, put on her coat, and was at the door of the flat, when a thought struck her. On Roses' dressing-table stood a little photograph of Frank – only a snapshot, not a studio portrait, but the face showed up clearly. Sally collected the photograph and put it in her bag. Rose would be furious, but that didn't matter, since they could scarcely be on worse terms than they were already. She only wished she had a photograph of Chris to show to Albert Harrington, too.

At the door of the flat Sally paused again. Well, why not? The need for action was driving her into a mood of recklessness. Why not go to Christian's flat first after all, challenge him if he were in, and if he was out, get the neighbour to let her in? It didn't really matter now what she did first: the main thing was to be doing something, to break out of this suffocating doubt and into the clear air of truth.

Chapter Fourteen

THE FINE SPELL had broken, and it was a heavy, overcast day with a feeling of dampness and chill in the air. Dead leaves from the horse chestnut trees lay piled up at the side of the paths in the park, and Sally shuffled through them. She had always loved walking among fallen leaves, but today the action was automatic and brought none of the usual contentment. As far as she was conscious of her surroundings at all, it was with a sense of the darkness and uncertainty of the winter to come. It was only her wild and reckless mood that was keeping intense depression at bay. Behind this great urge to action lay the fear that everything that mattered in her life was falling to pieces. Only one thing could save her: the absolute certainty that Christian was innocent and that he cared for her.

The middle bell was Christian's. Sally pushed at it firmly, without a second's hesitation. She had no idea what she was going to say. Nothing had been planned or rehearsed. There was only the determination to clear things up, and so intolerable was the feeling of frustration when nobody came to the door that she pressed the top bell. To be on the wrong side of a locked door – this seemed to Sally to sum up her situation exactly. Nobody came to answer the top bell either, but Sally continued to stare at the brown paint and the brass knocker and the letter-box as if hypnotized. A feeling of unreality came over her, as if she were living in a dream world in which nothing was stable, but all was in flux, as if solid things must dissolve, the door must give way and show her the truth.

Just as the bolt on the bathroom door had given way in that tossing ship ten years ago and shown her a truth that she could never suppress.

'Somebody want me?' said a slightly breathless voice behind her. 'Oh,' continued the plump fair woman from the top flat, 'you'll be wanting the doctor. Isn't he in?'

'He sent me along to fetch some books for him,' said Sally hurriedly, 'He said you'd be in and wouldn't mind letting me into the flat, as you kept his spare key.'

'That's right,' The plump woman opened the door. 'We keep one of his keys and he keeps one of ours.'

Sally followed her into the hall. She had not known what excuse she was going to make for getting in until the words actually came from her lips. It was as if her words and actions were being dictated to her moment by moment.

'You know I'm working for him now in the clinic, Mrs Martin?' she continued.

Mrs Martin, breathless again as she hurried up the stairs in front of Sally, indicated that she did know.

'We're so busy that we're working Saturday afternoons, too,' continued Sally, 'and there's a rather important legal point cropped up. I offered to come and fetch these books so he doesn't need to waste his time.'

Mrs Martin nodded again. 'I'll go and fetch the key,' she said when they reached the first-floor landing. 'Won't be long.'

The door of Christian's flat was painted brown like the

front door. It was shut now, but was about to be opened. Sally could not believe that it had all been so simple.

'I expect it will be in the living-room,' said Mrs Martin pushing open the door of the flat. 'That's where he keeps most of his books, though there are a few in the bedroom.'

Mrs Martin was walking about the flat as she talked, and Sally knew instantly first, that she had fully investigated its contents during Christian's absence, and second, that she intended to remain while Sally carried out her errand.

Had the errand been a genuine one, there would still have been every reason why Mrs Martin should remain. She recognized Sally, but she did not know her well, and she was responsible for the spare key. Sally studied the bookshelves while Mrs Martin said at length what a good neighbour the doctor was.

'I'm sure he is,' agreed Sally. She turned to the other bookcase. Whatever it was that was prompting her actions seemed temporarily to have deserted her. Somehow or other she must either get rid of Mrs Martin or get into the bedroom, for in the bedroom there must surely be some sort of personal possession; surely there must be a photograph somewhere. That there was nothing in the living-room, she knew from her previous visit. 'Ah – here's one of the books,' she said, taking down a thick volume entitled *The Law of Insanity*. 'I don't see the other anywhere.'

She moved back to the other bookcase that was nearer to the bedroom door. Mrs Martin had stopped talking for a moment and was looking out of one of the big sash windows, apparently interested in something outside in the street. Sally slipped through the bedroom door, went straight to the small bookcase that stood at the foot of the bed, picked out a volume at random, and then glanced quickly round the room. It was as simple and as impersonal as the living-room. The drawers of the big tallboy might yield something, but she had only seconds in which to look.

She pulled open the top drawer, saw some socks, some handkerchiefs, several small medicine bottles, and lying on top of a folded scarf was a small brown crocodile wallet. Sally picked it up and put it in her handbag, shut the drawer again and arrived a the door of the bedroom, triumphantly waving the book, at the same moment as Mrs Martin.

'Got it!' she cried. 'Thanks a lot, Mrs Martin. Sorry to have troubled you . . . No, I'd better not stay and have tea, thanks very much. He'll be waiting for these.'

She smiled at the neighbour and ran down the stairs. When she got out into the street she walked very quickly, longing to break into a run, but afraid that Mrs Martin might see her from the window and become suspicious. At the first side-street she turned and ran, and when she saw a cruising taxi she hailed it and told the driver she wanted to go to Prospect Terrace in Poplar.

'Cost you something, miss,' said the elderly man.

'I don't mind,' said Sally. 'I'm in a hurry to get there.'

The driver raised his eyebrows and pulled away. His looks said plainly that if well-dressed and well-brought-up young ladies wanted to waste their money on taxi-rides into the heart of London's dockland that was none of his business so long as they paid the fare. Sally looked in her purse, found three pounds six shillings and fivepence ha'penny, and decided that this would be enough for her purposes. Then she drew out the brown crocodile wallet.

I'm a thief, she said to herself as she opened it; I've actually stolen this.

But there was no feeling of guilt; only excitement. It was not a wallet for carrying money, but a small folder that could be opened out to stand up as a photograph frame. It contained two photographs, and Sally stared at them for so long that when she next looked up through the window of the taxi she saw that they were already nearing the City.

Each photograph was of two people – a man and a woman. The woman was the same, and it did not require much effort to guess who she was. Ralph's sister, Christian's wife, Louise. She was tall and slim, and wore a striped summer dress. From the house and garden in the background Sally judged that the pictures had been taken in Cape Town. Probably at Ralph's home, she added to herself. Looking at the face of Louise brought an odd little stab of pain. It's perfectly absurd, Sally told herself, to feel jealous of a woman who may not even be alive, who may even have been murdered, and just because the man who had been married to her had worshipped her. Perhaps even that was not true; perhaps it was Ralph's invention.

The photograph on the left showed Louise with Chris; on the right with Ralph. With the former she stood straight and stiff, a serious, almost sulky expression on her face, but with her brother she was laughing. They were arm-in-arm, half turned to each other, apparently enjoying a joke. It was they, and not the husband and wife, who looked the happy couple. Ralph looked very young and charming, but Sally believed she could detect weakness in the face.

At last Sally turned her full attention to the image of Christian. Like Louise, he was standing stiff and straight with his arms by his sides. He was wearing a light suit, and the eyes were concealed behind dark glasses. He looked even thinner than he did at present, but apart from this Sally could see little evidence that the picture had been taken many years ago. Perhaps it had not been. Perhaps Ralph was lying when he said his sister had disappeared a long time back and not been heard of since.

Sally took out the photograph of Frank that she had taken from Rose's dressing-table and compared it with that of Chris. Frank looked older of course, since it was a recent photograph, and in any case Frank was some years older than Chris, but there was no doubt that in height and build they were very similar. Much more alike, thought Sally, than she herself and Louise. It was not easy to assess ones' own appearance, but nevertheless she felt sure that Ralph had been exaggerating her own likeness to Christian's wife for some reason of his own. The picture of Frank was taken in half-profile so that the scar barely showed; any such mark on the other man's face was obscured by the glasses, but it would nevertheless be very easy to mistake the one face for the other.

The taxi wove through the City traffic and came out into a clear run along Commercial Road. Sally held the two photographs side by side in her lap, staring and staring at them, willing her memory to take a leap into certainty. It refused to do so. The taxi jolted at last to a halt. Sally glanced out of the window and gave a little involuntary cry. She was looking down on water, dark, dirty, frothy water.

175

'Swing bridge up,' said the driver, turning to face her. 'It really is an island. There's no other road. We'll have to wait, but it shouldn't take long.'

Sally returned all the photographs to her handbag, leaned back in the taxi, shut her eyes, and took deep breaths, trying to calm herself. She must not arrive for what could be a vital interview in a state of overwrought nerves.

'D'you know this area well?' she asked the driver presently.

'Not very well. We don't get many West End fares wanting to come down this way. I live in Balham myself.'

It was plain that he considered the South London suburb to be a cut above the East End.

'Then I suppose you wouldn't know if there's anywhere round here that I could get some tea,' said Sally. She had just realized that she was very hungry, having had nothing since some toast at breakfast-time, and it was now well on in the afternoon. It might be as well to fortify herself before tackling Albert Harrington. Of course, the old seaman might offer her some tea. If he's there, she added to herself, for the first time facing the possibility that he might be gone away, or out for the day, or even dead. The hopelessness that her impulsive actions had been holding at bay began to well up in her, and the drivers' reply did nothing to ease it.

'Doubt if there'd be anywhere round here where you'd fancy going for tea, miss,' he said discouragingly. 'Your best bet would be to walk through the tunnel under the river to Greenwich. You're more likely to find some-where that side.'

'A tunnel under the river?' In Sally's present state of

nerves this sounded almost as bad as crossing the river on a narrow footpath.

'That's right,' said the driver. 'There's a pedestrian subway. Never been in it myself but I believe it's quite clean and well-lit. Better sort of neighbourbood, Greenwich. Shouldn't advise you to hang about this side of the river for too long, miss. Certainly not after dark.'

After dark. After dark was very dark indeed in these days of blackout. Sally gave a little shudder. She was cold now, as well as hungry. For a moment she wished that she had taken her uncle's advice and waited for him to accompany her on this visit. He would be sitting by the open fire in the big sitting-room at Weir House now, in his usual chair, with Auntie Gertrude opposite and Sally's mother between them. They would be having tea and crumpets and anchovy toast and were probably talking about the evacuees. If she were there with them Sally knew she would feel irritated by their comfortable complacency, but in that moment of weakness she could not help wishing she were there, instead of going on what might well be a fool's errand to this remote part of London that felt so strange and threatening, with the road opening up to show unexpected stretches of river, and the cab-driver warning her against going into the local eating-places.

At least he was a friendly cab-driver, and Sally felt as if he was her only link with the London she knew. Suppose she were to come to some harm; suppose she were robbed or attacked in the blackout. Nobody would know where she had gone. Rose and Frank would not know. They were probably back in Park Mansions by now and wondering what had become of her. Rose would guess she had run away rather than face Frank. Where would she run to? Oxford and Weir House, of course. They would telephone and learn that she was not there, and the whole family would be alarmed, Uncle James in particular. Would he guess what she was doing? Would any of them think to telephone Ralph? She'd left his phone number on the pad in the hall, so that she could be rung at work if need be. And no doubt they could easily find Christian's number too.

What would Chris think if Rose were to speak to him and tell him Sally had disappeared? He'd ask her questions, and she would no doubt tell him about the quarrel and the accusation against Frank. And if Chris were at home he would have spoken to Mrs Martin and learnt that Sally had been there pretending to fetch some books – books that were lying beside her on the seat of the taxi and that she had almost forgotten. He would also have discovered that his photographs were missing, just as Rose would have discovered the loss of her picture of Frank. Would they all compare notes, exchange information? Would one or more of them come in search of her? And if so, who would it be, and would it be with goodwill and concern for her well-being, or with a very different motive – the motive of preventing her from learning whatever it was she might be going to learn from Albert Harrington?'

The bridge swung round and turned into roadway, and the taxi moved on, bringing with its movement some sense of relief to Sally. I must not think about anything else at all, she decided, deliberately suppressing the questions that had been flooding her mind; I must think only of talking to Albert Harrington.

'I am going to visit an old man who was in the crew of a ship I one travelled on,' she said to the taxi-driver. 'I want to see him urgently, but I don't know whether he'll be there or not. Will you wait while I find out? If he's not there, then I'll ask you to take me to Paddington Station.'

I'll go straight to Oxford if Albert Harrington's not there, decided Sally: I'll tell Uncle James everything, and leave it all to him.

When the taxi drew up at last at a little row of red-brick cottages across the road from a rather sad and neglected-looking little public garden, Sally had got to the point of hoping that there would be nobody in at No. 4. All the urgency of the search had left her. Even the quarrel with Rose had died down into a dull ache. She was tired and hungry and fearful, and was filled with an infantile yearning for food and rest and comfort and security. An image of the sitting-room at Weir House, with its crimson curtains and heavy furniture, hung in her mind like a vision of heaven.

She picked up Christian's two books, which seemed to have increased in weight since the start of the taxi-ride, told the driver she would not be long, and got out of the cab. No. 4 Prospect Terrace had a tiny front garden like its neighbours, but, unlike the neighbours, the garden was well cared for. There was a neatly clipped privet hedge and a pocket-handkerchief lawn, in the middle of which stood a rose-bush glowing with late scarlet blooms. The door was painted bright red, and the brass knocker, in the shape of an anchor, gleamed even on this dull afternoon.

Sally felt her spirits rise a little as she lifted her hand to knock. An image of the grey-haired man in his navy-blue

179

steward's uniform came into her mind, and for the first time since she had set out on this mission she felt that she was coming to visit someone she knew, coming to see an old friend.

The knock was answered by a short grey-haired woman wearing a white apron. A smell of baking, tantalizing Sally's hunger, came from within the house.

'Is this Mr Albert Harrington's home?' asked Sally.

The woman looked at her with a puzzled and rather anxious expression.

'What did you want with him?' she asked.

'I remember him from a voyage on one of the Cape and County boats when I was a child,' replied Sally. 'He was kind to me and now I'm in London I thought I'd like to see him again.'

She smiled at the grey-haired woman but received no answering smile. If anything, the other looked even more worried than before.

'Is he not well?' asked Sally. 'Have I come at a bad time?'

'Oh no, it's not that, although I can't say as he's ever well, not to say well, not since he had the stroke.'

'Stroke?' repeated Sally with a sinking of the heart. Had she come all this way, stolen those photographs, possibly put herself at risk, only to find that Albert Harrington, though alive, was rendered speechless, possibly even mindless, by a stroke?

'He feels awkward with strangers, you see,' went on the woman. 'He thinks they notice his face looks crooked, but it doesn't really. Or hardly at all. Only it worries him.'

'It won't worry me,' said Sally with her mind rolling back into hope again. 'I'd love to see him and talk to him. If he can talk all right. Can he talk all right?'

180

The answer to this question came not from the woman, but from the room to the right of the narrow entrance hall.

'Jeanie! Who's that, and why don't you hurry up and bring her in?'

The voice was clear, firm and impatient.

'Young lady to see you, Bert,' said the woman, putting her head round the door. 'Says she remembers you from one of the Cape boats.'

'Then bring her in. Bring her in, woman!'

'It's his legs, you see, it makes him so angry, not being able to walk,' explained Jeanie, who was presumably Mrs Harrington. 'Oh my goodness!' she went on. 'My cakes! They'll be ruined.'

She disappeared to the back of the house, and Sally put her head round the door of the little front parlour, said, 'I'm just paying the taxi – won't be a minute,' and withdrew.

'Don't let them overcharge you! All rogues – cabdrivers – rogues and thieves, the lot of them!'

Mr Harrington's voice came after her as she returned to the waiting driver.

'Six shillings, and here's one extra.' she said. 'Are you sure that's enough? After all, you've got to get back to the West End, and I don't expect you'll find any fares down here.'

The driver pocketed the money, stared at her, and slowly shook his head.

'You'll know me again,' said Sally, smiling.

'I'll know you again,' he said, continuing to shake his head. 'Twenty years come next summer I've been driving a cab in London, and that's the first time I've ever been told I'm not asking enough for the fare. Yes, miss, I'll know you again. Glad you've found your friends. You'll be all right now.'

'I'll be all right now,' said Sally. 'Thank you for taking care of me.'

The driver turned the cab quickly round and drove away, and Sally stood for a moment looking after it. She believed that she had indeed found a temporary haven, but nevertheless with the departure of the cab she felt as if her last link with her own familiar sphere had left her. Both Park Mansions and Weir House alike seemed to be in another world, as distant and unattainable as her own native land. She turned to look in the other direction before returning to the house and, saw between the bushes of the little garden a glimpse across the river to the Naval College at Greenwich, its stately white façade showing up against the green slope of Greenwich Park beyond.

The well-known London view comforted her and made her feel she was not so cut off after all. She and Charlie Brent had often talked of taking a boat down the river to Greenwich one weekend, but it had never come off. I expect they've stopped the pleasure boats now the war's on, thought Sally; we'll have to wait till peace, if it ever comes. It was several seconds before it occurred to her as extraordinary that she should be thinking of a trip to Greenwich with Charlie, whom she had more or less put out of her mind as far too young and immature for her now that she had come to know Chris. What strange jumps the mind made! It was as if her consciousness had for the moment returned to the months before her visit to Cape Town, and had picked up the interests and preoccupations of that time.

But it's got to go a lot further back than that now, she told herself as she came into the narrow hall of 4 Prospect Terrace; I wonder if Albert Harrington will remember me at all? After all, he must have made the trip dozens of times and talked to hundreds of passengers, so unless something unusual really did happen on the voyage of the *Cape St Vincent* . . .

Chapter Fifteen

'NOW, DON'T TELL ME,' said Albert Harrington. 'Let me see if I can remember.'

He sat in a black horsehair chair in a corner of the tiny room, with a rug over his knees in spite of the warmth of the coal fire.

'Let's look at you,' he continued holding out his left arm. 'Come over here into the light.'

Sally stood by the window and looked down on him. She remembered the beaky nose and the thick hair that grew into a peak at the centre of the forehead, giving the appearance of a bird. It had been grey then, and was white now. The face did indeed look rather lopsided, but the eyes were very alert.

'I'm sure you won't remember me,' she said. 'It was more than ten year ago, and I was only a child. I must have changed a lot. You've not changed much, Mr Harrington. I didn't know your name then, but you were kind to me. I'd been very seasick and had come up on deck when the boat stopped at Tenerife.'

The waving left arm signalled to her to come nearer. Sally knelt by the side of the horsehair chair, put her hands on the arm, and looked up into his face.

'Do you remember me, Mr Harrington?'

'I remember you. Oh yes, I remember you,' said the old man. His arm dropped and he leant back and shut his eyes. 'It's fate,' he said softly. 'It had to happen one day.'

Sally sat back on her knees and waited. The clink of crockery that came from the back of the house gave her the hope that she was going to be included in the meal that was being prepared. After a while Mr Harrington opened his eys and said: 'You've grown a bonny girl. You were a poor little waif on that ship.'

'Yes,' agreed Sally, and for a while they remained silent, staring at each other. Then Sally said: 'It seems as if you've guessed why I've come.'

The old man nodded. 'Yes, I've guessed. But why did you have to wait ten years?'

'Because—.' Sally broke off. Had he really guessed? Were they really talking about the same thing? 'Mr Harrington,' she said firmly, 'what was it about that last voyage of the *Cape St Vincent* that makes you remember it so well?'

'You'll have to ask Jeanie to talk.' The old man shut his eyes again. 'It's been too much for me. I'm too tired.'

Sally got to her feet and at the same moment Mrs Harrington came into the room carrying a tray.

'You'll stop and have a cup with us, Miss—', she began.

'Livingstone,' said Sally helping to set out the tea things on the table, which was covered by a shining white damask cloth.

'Livingstone. That's right. Livingstone. Funny that I should forget the name.'

Sally paused with a willow-pattern teacup in her hand

and stared at the weather-beaten old face of Jeanie Harrington.

'How do you know who I am?' she asked, and even as she spoke she had a tantalizing sense of familiarity, as if she had lived through a similar situation before. Was it the voice, or the face, or the fact that the woman was handling crockery and cutlery that produced this spur to the memory? Sally did not know. She only knew that the puzzle seemed to be clicking together at such a rate that her thoughts could not digest it. 'You brought me beef tea,' she said to Mrs Harrington. 'You were always bringing me cups of beef tea.'

'That's right. There was nothing else we could do for you.'

'Were you married then?' Sally looked from the old steward to the old stewardess and back again.

'No,' said Mrs Harrington. 'We married two years later, after Bert retired. But we were courting, you might say, on *St Vincent*'s last voyage. That's why he came to me for help.' She looked across at her husband. 'You want me to tell her, Bert?'

'Yes,' said Mr Harrington. 'She must have found something out, otherwise she wouldn't be here. You do the talking, love. I'll chip in when I need to. And give us some tea first.'

Mrs Harrington supplied all three of them with strong tea and rock buns hot from the oven. Sally ate and drank and felt better, and when it seemed as if the old stewardess was not going to begin, she said: 'I don't really know anything at all, but I've got a memory of that voyage that has frightened me for all these years, but I've never been sure whether it really happened or not. I met somebody recently – two people in fact – who started my memory up again, and I've been trying to find out what really did happen. I got your address from the Cape and County offices' – she turned to Mr Harrington – 'because I thought you might be able to help me discover the truth. There was a man I saw on that boat whom nobody else seems to have seen, and I believe he could be one of the two people I've mentioned. I've got their photographs here, and I wanted to ask you if you recognized any of them.'

The two old people exchanged looks. Albert Harrington put his teacup down on the little table beside him and said: 'Let's have a look at them.'

Sally got up and knelt by his chair again while he studied the three photographs for what seemed a very long time.

'Come over here, Jeanie,' he said at last.

Mrs Harrington got up from the tea-table, and Sally moved aside to let her come close to the black horsehair chair.

'That's him all right, isn't it?' said the old man pointing at the crocodile wallet.

Sally craned her head to try to see which picture he was indicating. It was impossible to tell.

'Yes, that's him,' agreed Mrs Harrington. 'That's Dr Hall.'

'God rot him!' exclaimed Albert Harrington, so violently that Sally gave a little jump.

'Dr Hall?' she said 'I don't know any of these people as Dr Hall.'

'Changed his name, no doubt,' said Albert Harrington bitterly. 'Can't change his conscience though.'

Sally put a hand to her head. It felt as if it were bursting. One moment the jigsaw puzzle seemed to be nearing completion, and the next moment all the pieces were jumbled up again in a worse muddle than before. Dr Hall, she said to herself; I've seen that name recently. Where? Dr Hall . . .

Suddently it came to her like a flash of lightning that she knew nothing whatever about Christian except what he himself had told her. How did she even know that Rudolph Christian Hofmeyr was his real name? For all she knew it had once been Hall.

Hall. Of course. Captain Hudson's diary. The new medico. Hall. But Rose had said . . .

'Please,' begged Sally, her thoughts reeling, '*Please* tell me which of these two you knew as Dr Hall?'

Jeanie Harrington stepped aside and Sally came close enough to the old man to see at which photograph he was pointing.

'That one, of course, the smarmy devil,' he said.

The short stubby index finger was placed at the bottom of the right-hand photograph. Sally rubbed at her forehead again.

'He must have changed his name' she said in a dazed voice. 'I know him as Dr Curtis.'

'Curtis Hall. That's right,' said Albert Harrington.

'Oh. I see.' Sally's mind jumped back to the ivory paperknife on Ralph's desk with the initials RCH. Ralph Curtis Hall. He had simply dropped the last name. And because the initials were the same as Christian's . . .

'Do you know the woman he is with?' she asked.

The old steward shook his head. 'Never seen her. Jeanie?'

'Never seen her,' said Mrs Harrington.

'You're quite sure she was not on the *Cape St Vincent*?' said Sally.

'Quite, quite sure,' said the two old people in unison.

Then it looks as if Louise is out of it, thought Sally: she can't have been the body in the porthole. That was only Ralph trying to cast suspicion on Chris. With an effort she brought her thoughts under control and tried to take in what she had heard. It looked as if Ralph Curtis, or Ralph Curtis Hall, was now to be cast in the role of villain, which Sally was very glad to believe, but on the other hand there was no doubt at all that he was not the man she had seen in the bathroom. In the light of fresh revelation she would be willing to revise her opinion about practically everything, but that was one fact that could not be altered.

It had not been Ralph.

Then it must have been Christian.

'Do you remember ever having seen either of these other two men?' she asked.

The crocodile wallet and the framed photograph of Frank Sedgemore lay on the brown rug. Jeanie Harrington leant over and placed the framed photograph over the picture of Ralph and Louise, overlapping the figure of Louise in the other picture so that the images of Christian and Frank were side by side. Husband and wife stared at the two pictures, looking from one to the other, frowning in concentration.

'That looks like the man,' said Jeanie, pointing to Frank.

'No, I think it's the other.' The stubby forefinger was placed on the photograph of Christian.

'What man? Where did you see him?' cried Sally.

They took no notice of her but continued to argue between themselves.

'I saw more of him than you did,' said Albert Harrington.

'When?' demanded his wife.

'When I was trying to find out what had happened to Lisa. He kept trying to get away, but I didn't let him. I blocked the way down from the boat deck, and he just had to talk. Said Lisa was Dr Hall's pigeon, not his.'

'What time of day was this?' asked Mrs Harrington.

'Oh – latish. But if you're thinking it was too dark for me to see him properly, I tell you it wasn't. I saw him all right, and I tell you that's the man.' Albert Harrington prodded at the photograph of Christian. 'That's him. That's the one,' he repeated, becoming more and more agitated.

'But what had he done?' cried Sally. 'And who is Lisa?'

Still they took no notice of her. Jeanie Harrington, as excited now as her husband, was leaning over the side of his chair and pointing at the picture of Frank. 'It's this one, sure as eggs is eggs. Looks older, but it must have been taken later. It's this one, Bert, and there's no need for you to be so pig-headed about it. You only saw him in the dark. I saw him on the stairs with Dr Hall. I saw him much clearer than you.'

'But you wouldn't have so much cause to notice him. You didn't know then what was going to happen to Lisa. Don't cross me so, Jeanie. I know I'm right.'

The old man was becoming breathless in his agitation, and his wife, too, seemed for a moment to have run out of steam. In the temporary lull Sally put her question again.

'Please, please tell me,' she said, 'what are you talking about. Who is Lisa?'

They both stared at her as if they had forgotten she was there.

'Who is Lisa?' she asked again.

'She doesn't know,' said Albert Harrington turning back to his wife. 'Her having all these pictures, I thought she must have found out. She doesn't know, Jeanie.' His voice sounded weak and disappointed. The burst of excitement seemed to have exhausted him.

'But I do know something, truly I know something,' said Sally. 'Only tell me first – who is Lisa?'

'We'd better all have another cup of tea,' said Mrs Harrington, returning to the table. 'You keep quiet, Bert. You've had more excitement than is good for you. Lisa,' she went on turning to face Sally, 'is Bert's daughter. Not mine. Bert's daughter.'

Chapter Sixteen

THE DULL AFTERNOON began to darken into twilight as Mrs Harrington told her story.

'Let's have a light, lass,' grumbled Mr Harrington. 'We're not so poor that we can't afford a bit of gas.'

'If I light the lamp I'll have to do the blackout, Bert,' said his wife.

'Then do the blackout, do the blackout,' he cried. 'Get it over with or we'll have old Nosey Parker round making an excuse to find out who our visitor is.'

Mrs Harrington got up and pulled a thick black curtain across the little square window, checked carefully to make sure there was no crack, and then covered it with a cheerful red and white checked curtain.

'Our neighbour fixed up the extra rail,' she explained to Sally. 'He's an air-raid warden and often comes in to give me a hand, now Bert can't do much. We've got to be very careful here, he says. Being right by the docks, you see. They'll have a go at the docks, he says. Jerry's bound to have a go at the docks. Some folks have gone away, but we've nowhere to go, and anyway it would break his heart –' and she nodded towards her husband, now resting with closed eyes – 'to have to leave this house. All the years he's longed for a little place of his own and a bit of earth to plant a rose-bush . . . Oh no, we'll never leave, Bert and I. Not if it was raining bombs like cats and dogs.'

Sally watched the little woman bustle about the room, put an extra cushion behind Albert's head, and fill up the teapot from the kettle that was simmering on the hob. She felt as if she were in a dream, as if the cosy little room with the glowing fire and the hum of the gas-lamp and the two old people and the cheerful tea-table was some vision of her imagination, and that any moment now she would come back to real life. When had it stopped and turned into a dream? In London in the autumn of 1939, a dark and threatening background to her own dark and apprehensive thoughts? Or had her real life stopped a few weeks earlier, when she had sat with her aunt and her cousins in the garden of their new bungalow on Constantia Heights, looking at one of the splendid views of the Cape Peninsula and discussing whether or not she ought to return to England, with the war clouds gathering? Was that the reality to which she would awaken after this dream? Or was it even further back – on a tired old ocean liner making her last voyage in Atlantic waters?

Mrs Harrington filled up Sally's cup and cut her a slice of seed-cake. I don't remember her face, thought Sally, but I remember the way she fussed over me in that cabin. Like a nurse in starched uniform.

'Bert's first wife was Portuguese,' said Mrs Harrington in a matter-of-fact way. 'She came from the Canary Islands. Grand Canary originally, but Bert actually met her at Tenerife when she was working in a café. They never really had a home. You don't, you know, when you're at sea. Sometimes she got a job in the cook's galley so they could be together on board – not that you've ever got any time to see each other, the way they work you! They had one child, a daughter, Lisa. Bert used to worry about her after her mother died, wished he could keep an eye on her.'

'No life for a decent girl, those harbour cafés.' interposed Mr Harrington abruptly.

'No life,' agreed Jeanie. 'But what could he do? He said he'd get a job ashore, but she didn't want to come to England – said it was too cold and foggy – and he couldn't find a job in Cape Town – it isn't so easy when you're getting on – and he didn't want to stop in Tenerife. Never got on with his in-laws. Bert's got a temper, though you wouldn't think it.' Jeanie glanced at her husband fondly. 'So Lisa hung around in Cape Town for some of the time, and in Tenerife for the rest of the time, and the Lord knows what she got up to there.'

'The Lord knows and you know too,' said Mr Harrington. 'Up to no good.'

'It was the men, you see,' explained Mrs Harrington to Sally. 'They were all after her. If you'd ever seen her you'd know why. Did you ever see her?'

'I – I don't really know,' faltered Sally, hoping that Mrs Harrington would finish her own tale before Sally was asked for hers.

'Black hair and eyes, lovely complexion. She was all her mother, nothing of poor old Bert in her except the pigheadedness. She had that all right. Mind you, she could deal with the men. She fancied them, but she was choosy. No rough young seamen for Lisa. She liked the gents, the smooth types. And they liked her. Always hoping one of them would marry her, she was. That's where she was wrong. They wasn't going to marry her,

194

not that type. They'd have what they wanted and then be off. Why she never got into trouble before, that's what beats me.'

'Got into trouble?' Sally, listening eagerly, found in this phrase a clue as to what was to come.

'That's right,' said Mrs Harrington. 'That's why Lisa stowed away on the *St Vincent* when she stopped at Tenerife on her last voyage. Came aboard with the rest of the mob and hid in one of the lifeboats until the ship sailed. Lisa knew her way about all right, and knew what to do. Bert had gone ashore and couldn't find her anywhere, and came back worried to death. Got the fright of his life when she suddenly popped up in the pantry that night. That's when he called me – we was good friends then, sort of courting – and asked what he was to do with her. I said I'd put her in an empty cabin on C Deck and bring her meals there. I could manage all right without anyone knowing. She'd have to pop out to the bathroom sometimes, but if she was careful no one would see. You never saw her, did you?'

Sally shook her head. It was true, she thought, that she had never seen Lisa Harrington alive.

'I didn't think so, and I knew your ma and your sister never saw her. They were much too taken up with the party. Little they worried about you lying there so sick, poor little mite! They'd certainly not trouble themselves looking for stowaways.'

'I suppose she was pregnant,' said Sally, as Mrs Harrington seemed to have come to a pause in her narrative.

'That's right. Three months gone. Wouldn't tell her dad who the father was, but swore he was on that ship and

195

she was going to challenge him. Blackmail's a risky business, Bert told her. You be careful, my girl. You're not meant to be on this ship at all, and nobody knows you're here, only Jeanie and me. Don't you go sticking your neck out. There's lots of things can happen on a ship that nobody ever knows about. There's people can disappear off ships and nobody ever knows. Just think of all that sea out there and all the secrets it's hiding. One dead body more or less is nothing in all that sea. That's what Bert said to her.'

'Didn't she realize?' asked Sally, glancing at Albert Harrington, who was still sitting with his eyes closed.

'Thought she knew best, of course,' said Jeanie. 'Stubborn as a mule, Lisa, when she'd made up her mind. He'll marry me or else, she said. Or else what? I asked. Or else it'll be the worse for him, she said. He's blotted his copybook already, and he's not in the sort of job where people stand for it. Got a reputation to lose, this one has. And she laughed so loud, we was down in the cabin then, that I was afraid someone would hear, but seemingly nobody did. That was Christmas Eve in the early morning. All fast asleep, I expect you were.'

'What happened then?' asked Sally.

'Bert and I talked to her a bit more – we was scared every minute that someone would find her or wonder why we weren't about our duties, but we couldn't move her. Bert said something about trying to get rid of the baby. I didn't like that. It's not right, and I didn't like it, but that's the way men always think, and she said she'd thought of that but didn't want to try anything risky. So Bert said, Don't you know of any doctor? And she laughed again and said, All right, I'll ask the doctor. That's an idea. I'll ask the doctor. Just you send the doctor down to me and I'll ask him. Well, I didn't much like this, but Bert said, why not, Dr Hall was only a young chap and hadn't made many trips, but he seemed to know what he was about. There'd been an appendix case – one of the men in the engine-room – and Dr Hall had done an emergency operation and made a very good job of it. I'll say that for him – he was a good doctor so long as he kept off the bottle.'

'Good doctor!' Albert Harrington roused himself. 'He was a . . .'

The voice dropped to an inaudible mumbling, and Sally guessed that he was murmuring epithets that he did not consider suitable for a young lady's ears.

'At any rate, we didn't think he would tell on us,' went on Mrs Harrington. 'Whatever he said to Lisa, we felt sure he'd not let on that she was stowed away on the boat. And he didn't tell anybody else, only this man he said he knew who'd help hide her in the first-class till we docked at Southampton. Getting her ashore, you see. That was a problem. It's different at the English ports from what it is at Tenerife. Leave it to me, he said. We'll fix it, he says. Leave it to us. That was after he'd talked to Lisa, and when I managed to pop in to her with a bit to eat she waved it aside and said; nothing to eat here – I'm going to be eating better than that, and laughed again. What are you doing? I asked, and she laughed some more and said; That'll be telling. Don't you worry, Ma. I'll be all right. I've got it all fixed. And that was the last I saw of her, and the last Bert saw too, but I did see the doctor going down to C Deck a little later together with this man here –' and she picked up the photograph of Frank that was now lying on the table – 'and I tried to speak to Dr Hall, but he simply smiled and put a finger to his lips. And later on, well, Bert and I asked Dr Hall where Lisa was, for she'd disappeared from the cabin, and he said; She's all right, she's being looked after up in the first class. I told you we'd attend to it. He was in a hurry then – he wanted to get back to the party. We still didn't like it much, but we supposed it was all right, and we was talking it over in the pantry when you range the bell from your cabin and I came down and found you very poorly and feverish, talking about having seen a man in the bathroom. I didn't know what to make of that, but I called Dr Hall – he didn't like coming; he wanted to stay at the party, and he'd already been having a few, I could see that. You went on crying and screaming, and he took a look at you and said; Very feverish, the child's delirious, not much we can do. Nothing we can give her, he says, as she'll only go and bring it up again.'

The old stewardess paused for a moment and Sally asked: 'Didn't you believe I'd really seen someone?'

'I didn't know what to believe,' was the reply. 'I was that worried about Bert and Lisa I didn't know what to think. I didn't feel up to looking after a sick child at that moment, and that's the truth, and what your mother was about, gallivanting off to parties and leaving you like that—'

'I was all right,' said Sally in a low voice. 'I wanted to be alone. Truly.'

The old couple exchanged glances. 'When people have got the money and the time to look after their children,' began Mrs Harrington.

'Not like us,' said her husband bitterly.

'Please,' begged Sally. 'Please go on telling me.'

'There's nothing much more to tell.' Albert Harrington

took up the tale. 'I tried to get Dr Hall to tell me where Lisa was, and all he said was that this man was taking care of her – that fellow there, the one standing with the woman.' He waved his arm in the direction of the photographs lying on the table. 'I said I wanted to see him, and Dr Hall said no, better keep right away, it'd only arouse suspicions. I wasn't supposed to be in the first-class, you see, but I didn't think anyone'd mind. Captain Hudson and me, we was old friends. He'd had me to his farewell party, earlier in the voyage. I even thought I'd tell the Captain, tell him the whole story, how Lisa had come aboard. He knew I had trouble with Lisa. He might've understood. He might've helped me. And then I thought, no, better not. Lisa said the father of her baby was somewhere on the boat. Maybe it was one of the officers. Maybe it was a decent man who'd get into trouble if it all came out. Maybe it was a friend of the captain's. You see, lassie –' and the old man leaned forward towards Sally in a confidential manner – 'what we thought then, Jeanie and I, was that Lisa had asked the doctor to get rid of the baby for her, and that he'd done it, and that that had shut her mouth. We thought she'd realized after all what a risky business blackmail is, and that she had decided to keep quiet if only she could get rid of the baby. So although we were very worried we still didn't think anything really bad had happened to her, and if she came ashore safely at Southampton – well, she'd have learnt her lesson, I reckoned, and maybe I'd get her to see sense and settle down somewhere and make a decent sort of a home for her old Dad when he was ashore.'

'It was only another two days to Southampton,' said

Mrs Harrington, 'but the night before we docked Bert and I talked again, and he said he'd like to see Lisa. He was afraid something might have gone wrong when they were getting rid of the baby, and he didn't trust the doctor, he said, and he was determined to find this man in the first-class who was supposed to be looking after her and to find out what was happening. He asked some of his mates and somebody said there were several people among the passengers whom it might be, and they'd keep a lookout, but it was very stormy those last few days and there was hardly anyone in the saloon at meals. People were sticking to their cabins, and some of them had put notices up not to disturb. And we was so busy ourselves with so many people being sick – and trays and things, and the bells never stopped ringing – anyway, Bert did get a chance to go in search later that night, and that's when he had this conversation he's mentioned, and this man said don't worry, your daughter's all right, and what could we do? If we raised a hue and cry the whole ship would know. So when we docked we tried our best to see the passengers leaving, but we was for ever being sent for to do this, that and the other, and of course we missed some of them. So I said to Bert, she'll turn up, we'll find her at your brother's in London. This house belonged to Bert's brother, you see, that's why we've got it. But she never came. We never saw any more of her. And Bert wrote to Dr Hall – it had to be care of the Cape and County, because we didn't have his address – and we did get a letter back, months later, posted in Cape Town. He was very sorry, he said, but he couldn't help us. He'd handed the charge of Lisa over to this other man, and knew nothing about her.'

'Didn't you make any more attempts to track down the other man?' asked Sally.

'I did that,' said the old man. 'I talked to all my mates on the *St Vincent* until they were sick to death of us. She's given you the slip, they said. Told me I'd fussed over the girl so much that she'd decided she'd had enough. Probably got herself a sugar daddy, they said, probably queening it somewhere in South America. That's the way they talked. That's what happens to the likes of us when we need help. If she'd been an heiress now, or even a young lady like yourself, they'd have had Scotland Yard on the job. But what was the use of me going to the police? Evidence? We'd not enough evidence to convict a fly. Jeanie and me on one side, and Lisa's bad reputation that there'd be dozens to swear to, what was that against Doctor Curtis Bloody Hall and his gang of smooth-tongued hypocrites!'

'Mr Harrington.' Sally got up, moved to the old man's chair, knelt down and took his left hand in both her own. 'Mr Harrington, I believe I can tell you what happened to your daughter. But whether it will bring you any comfort I don't know.'

'It'll be comfort,' he said grimly, 'if it's the truth. I don't believe in miracles. All I want is the truth. It's the not knowing that takes the stuffing out of you. It's the nagging doubt that strikes you dead at the heart.'

'Oh yes, oh yes indeed!' cried Sally, feeling the tears start to her eyes. 'It's the doubt that kills you.'

For a moment she was too overcome to speak. It looked as if her own doubts had been resolved at last. It must have been Christian on the boat, in spite of Jeanie Harrington's identification of Frank. Of course it was

201

Christian. But what part had he played? Whose was the baby, Ralph's or Christian's? Had Ralph carried out the bungled abortion and then begged Christian to get rid of the body and back up his own lies? Or had Christian done the lot?

Please God, cried Sally very softly under her breath; Don't let it turn out that he did it all.

'Mr Harrington,' she began, 'on that day of the fancy dress party—'

She was interrupted by a loud knocking at the door of the tiny house. They've found me, said the voice of fear in her mind; they've tracked me down. What will they do? Murder all three of us? Any one of us alone is no threat, but the three of us here with our pooled knowledge . . .

Mrs Harrington had got up and gone to the door. 'Hullo, Willie!' she called out loudly. 'What's up, then? Not showing a light, are we?

'Not showing a light, nor showing a leg either,' said a loud male voice. 'I just looked in to see if there's anything you need. But it seems you've got company.'

'I've got company,' called out Albert Harrington from his chair. 'Much better company than yours, Willie Brunton! I've got a very nice young lady here, so don't you go bringing my old woman into the room!'

After a few more exchanges of this sort the neighbour departed.

'Where were we?' asked Mrs Harrington returning to the tiny parlour.

'She says she's going to tell us what happened to Lisa,' said Albert. 'And I believe she will, too. I believe she's been sent.' He stared at Sally broodingly. 'It's Providence, that's what it is. It was meant to happen this way.

Takes away our daughter and sends us this little girl instead.'

He must be seeing me as the child in the deckchair, thought Sally, just as I'm seeing him in his navy-blue uniform.

'When they were all at the fancy dress party I came out of the cabin to go to the bathroom,' she said quickly. 'The ship was rolling dreadfully. I had to cling to the rail. The bathroom door was shut, but the boat went right over as if it was never going to come up again, and the bolt must have slipped and the door burst open. And I saw a man pushing the body of a woman through the porthole.'

A little sound burst from Mrs Harrington. Sally hurried on without looking at her. 'I could only see her legs and her skirt. It was red, and she was wearing black patent leather shoes.'

'Ah!' The exclamation came in the form of a long-drawn-out note from Albert Harrington. 'Ah! That's right. That was Lisa. That was my daughter.'

Mrs Harrington got up from the table and went and stood by the side of his chair, putting a hand on his shoulder. 'You did say you wanted to know the truth, love,' she said.

'That's right. I want the truth. I'm not complaining. So they killed her between them or one or the other of them, and had to get rid of her body.' Suddenly he thumped on the arm of the chair and leant forward, breaking away from his wife's restraining hand: 'Which was the man?' he cried, glaring at Sally. 'Which of them was the man?'

'I – I don't know,' she faltered. Then she said more firmly. 'It wasn't the man you call Dr Hall. I do know that.'

Albert Harrington leant back again with an expression almost of disappointment on his face. 'That doesn't mean he didn't do the killing, though,' he muttered. 'Could have got his mate to do the rest of the dirty work.'

'It was one of the other two?' Mrs Harrington passed a hand gently over the old man's hair as she looked at Sally.

'I think so.'

'Which one of them?'

'I'm not sure. They're so alike. I don't really know. It was only for a second or two, and I was so sick . . . I just don't know,' said Sally.

But that's a lie, she added to herself; of course I know it was Christian. Mrs Harrington thinks she recognizes Frank, but it can't have been Frank. He's nothing to do with it. Of course it was Christian. But he didn't do the abortion. Surely, surely he didn't do the abortion. Ralph did that and bungled it and panicked and sought Christian's help . . . and because he was Louise's brother and Christian loved Louise . . . He did it for loyalty . . . it wasn't a bad motive . . . it was from loyalty . . .

'Well I think it was that one in the silver frame,' said Jeanie Harrington. Then she stepped back quickly as Albert began to thump on the arm of the chair again.

'What does it matter which of 'em it was?' he cried. 'Villains, the lot of them! They killed my daughter. And they got away with it. How did you get these pictures, anyway?' he added, looking keenly at Sally. 'Are they friends of yours?'

'Not exactly,' said Sally. It was the question she had been dreading, and it was surprising that it had not been asked before now. But they had all three been so deeply entrenched in the past that even she had come close to forgetting her present situation.

'How do you mean, not exactly?' pressed Mr Harrington. 'You said you knew Dr Hall, and you must know the others or you wouldn't have their pictures.'

'Well, actually I stole them' said Sally.

'Stole them!' The two old people exclaimed together, and then Albert gave a little chuckle and said: 'Nicked them, did you? That's my girl. She's got spunk. I told you, Jeanie, that child's got spunk for all she's such a poor little thing.'

It occurred to Sally again that there was some confusion in the old man's feelings, if not in his mind, and that he was in some way regarding her as a substitute for his lost daughter.

'That's all very well,' said Mrs Harrington sharply, 'but what about when they find out the pictures are missing? If they're not exactly friends of yours, then what are they?'

'The man in the frame,' said Sally, 'whom you think pushed Lisa's body into the sea, is the man my sister is engaged to. You remember my sister?'

Yes, they remembered her sister; always tagging round after Mum. Sally explained yet again how she had recognized Frank when she came back from Cape Town.

'There you are, you see!' cried Mrs Harrington triumphantly. 'I knew that was the one!'

'I see,' said Albert thoughtfully. 'So that's what started you off. Didn't want your sister to marry him. Have you told her?'

'Not till today. We had a terrible quarrel and she said she was going to tell him I'd accused him of murder.'

Mr and Mrs Harrington stared at each other and then at Sally. 'That's not spunk,' said Albert, 'that's just plumb crazy. It's lucky for you it's not the man. Case of mistaken identity.'

'How do you know?' demanded Jeanie.

'Stands to reason,' said Albert. 'There's a picture of Dr Bloody Hall with a woman and there's a picture of another feller with the same woman. So they must be connected, see?'

'I suppose so,' said Mrs Harrington reluctantly.

'Course it's so, ain't it?' Albert Harrington turned to Sally. 'Course you know who killed my Lisa. You don't want to know. That's what it is. Got a hold on you, has he, this feller?'

'Not exactly,' said Sally, getting up from the table, and looking round the tiny room as if she felt trapped there. The thought of explaining about Christian to this couple was so daunting that she wanted to run away. It was this instinct for flight, combined with the fact that she was nearest to the door of the room when the loud knock came, that led her to rush out into the hall several seconds ahead of Mrs Harrington.

She pulled open the front door and saw a tall figure in the dimness.

'Shut the door – you're showing light,' said a low voice.

As if hypnotized Sally pulled the door shut behind her. A hand reached out for hers and pulled her along the short path to the pavement. In the faint glow from the dimmed streetlamp she saw the outline of a car – a sports car, open-topped. Her will and her powers of reasoning returned and she began to struggle. She opened her mouth to scream but only a strangled sound came out.

She felt damp on her face and heard the sound of falling water. In a split second all the horror of her life seemed to clash together and wipe the heart out of her. Then her mind cleared, and she knew it was raining heavily and that the other sound she had heard was the swish of tyres on a wet road. She fought with greater strength against the arms that were forcing her into the sports car and opened her mouth and heard clearly her own scream for help.

After that it was all confusion. There were shouts and men fighting in the darkness, and the hands holding her let go and she fell back, dizzy, against something half tough, half yielding. It was the privet hedge encircling the little garden, she realized as she pulled herself upright. 'Are you all right?'

Someone was standing near her, holding her arm gently. It was a familiar voice; an educated English voice with the merest trace of a South African accent.

'Yes. Thanks, Ralph,' she said.

But Dr Curtis had already left her side. There were more shouts and more fighting, and then a roar from the engine of the sports car.

'Quick – my taxi!' shouted Ralph. 'After him!'

The young taxi-driver got back into his seat, and Sally followed Ralph and another man into the cab. He had on an air-raid warden's steel helmet. The neighbour, she thought. Willy Brunton. He must have heard me. It was extraordinary how clear her mind was now. Christian had guessed where she was and what she was doing and had taken Ralph's car, and Ralph had followed him in this taxi, and she probably owed her life to Ralph.

I'm not grateful. I can't feel grateful, she said to herself. I'd rather be dead.

'Blimey!' cried the cab-driver. 'He's going to rush the bridge!'

The taxi slowed down; the sports car raced ahead. The red lights were flashing, warning that the roadway was turning round to let a ship through; dimmed lights because of the blackout, but clear enough warning for drivers.

'He'll never make it,' said the cab-driver.

Ralph and the other man were leaning out of the window of the cab. Sally sank back with her eyes closed. Please God, she murmured to herself; please God, let him not be caught.

'He's on it!' cried one of the men. 'He's on the bridge!'

'Is he stopping?'

'Can't see – can't see a bloody thing.'

There was a loud screech of brakes and then the sports engine roared again. The cab-driver and the two men in the taxi jumped out and ran forward. Their shouts mingled with the shouts of the men working the bridge, and those on the ship coming through.

Sally heard it all, but kept her eyes closed. Please God, let him not be caught, she prayed.

'My God!' In a sudden lull one of the voices rang out loud and clear. It was Ralph's. 'My car!'

There was something of anguish in this last cry. Then the shouting began again, but much louder than the shouting was the tremendous roar of the powerful engine, and then came a split second when all sounds ceased, and then a great splash, and then silence for several seconds.

Sally put her hands over her face. Thank God, she muttered. She felt dampness on her eyes; she had not known she was crying.

'Lisa,' she whispered to herself. 'Albert's daughter Lisa. When Lisa went into the water she didn't make such a splash.'

Chapter Seventeen

'I'M NOT HAVING any argument whatever,' said Ralph.

They were standing in his sitting-room above the surgery. The room was in better order now, with the books unpacked and the pictures on the walls.

'You are not travelling to Oxford or anywhere else tonight,' he went on. 'You are sleeping here. On the surgery couch or in one of the upstairs rooms. Just as you like. But you're going to have a strong sedative and at least ten hours' sleep. That's doctor's orders. You're in a state of shock following extreme tension and anxiety. I'm phoning your uncle, and I'm phoning your sister, and tomorrow morning you can decide which of them you want to go to and I'll take you. Now sit down while I make tea.'

Sally sat down. Her little burst of spirit was gone. She was indeed exhausted, cold, shivering, barely able to stand. In a state of shock, as Ralph had said. She had to be grateful to him, she supposed, and in her present condition she had to be somebody's patient, but oh, how she hated him. He had killed all her hopes and dreams. She felt as if he had killed Christian. As indeed he had. He had caused Christian's death. Of course it had to be that way. She had herself prayed that Christian would escape, and in a way he had escaped – escaped by drowning. Sally didn't blame Ralph for that. It was not the man who had driven Ralph's sports car into the waters of the Thames whom Sally was mourning; it was the man whom Sally had believed she could love. That was the man whom Ralph had destroyed, and Sally could not forgive him.

She didn't want to know about it, and yet she knew she could not rest until she knew it all. Ralph knew that, too. Oh yes, he was a good doctor all right; of the mind as well as of the body. He understood her needs, and he'd carry out the job of first aid, and he'd restore her to her own people as the Sally they knew, no longer tormented by doubts, no longer blazing away to find the truth; sound in mind and body, but with a deadness at the heart.

'Thanks,' said Sally and sipped the sweet, weak tea.

'I like the pictures,' she said a little later.

'Yes,' said Ralph, 'I know Arnold quite well. These are going to be worth quite a lot of money one day.'

Typical of him, sneered Sally's mind; he doesn't think of the art; he thinks only of the money. Hateful man. But he's an honest man. Oh yes, it's he, and not Christian, who's the honest man, and who was bending his honesty out of loyalty. Honest Englishman. Kiss the Union Jack. Down with the lesser breeds – and that goes for Afrikaners as well as natives. Oh yes. I believe him, all right. I know it's true. Everything he's going to say is true.

'I did try to warn you,' said Ralph, 'but I didn't do it properly. I was still hoping it wouldn't come to a head. When he was well he was the finest doctor I've ever known. But there were times when he was not really sane. You realize that, of course.'

'Yes,' said Sally.

'He did make a murderous attack on Louise. Mind you, she'd given him cause. As I told you. But it wasn't the only time. There'd been other women he'd attacked – fortunately nothing that ended seriously. Louise ran away with an American and is still there as far as I know. He did worship her. And you are like her. That's what was worrying me so much. That, and your obvious partiality for him.'

'What about the *Cape St Vincent* voyage?' asked Sally. She didn't want to hear Ralph talking about her own partiality for Christian.

'That's where I'm hoping you'll clear something up for me,' said Ralph, 'because I still haven't got the full story. I guessed you were in even greater danger than I'd thought when Chris started raving about the Harringtons. We came in to his place together, and found that you'd been there and taken the photographs. It was obvious what you were up to. I tried to stop him and we had a fight in the car . . . you know what happened then. I'll tell you quickly all I know about the *Cape St Vincent* voyage and you will fill in the vital gap for me. Bert will have told you how Lisa stowed away and he asked me to see her. I knew Lisa, but I'd never slept with her. Too risky. Didn't want to catch anything. But of course the Harringtons thought the baby was mine. Lisa deliberately made them think so without actually saying it. She was a devil. She told me the kid was Chris's. She knew he was on the boat and she was going to tackle him.

'I didn't know whether to believe it or not. It could

212

have been Chris's, I supposed. We never talked about that sort of thing, and he'd just got engaged to Louise and was coming to England to see about taking up a hospital appointment in London and setting up a home for her there before coming back to Cape Town to marry her. He was doing well, and was in funds then. I'd taken on the ship's doctoring more or less for a lark before settling down. I didn't like this Lisa business. It smacked of blackmail to me. Somehow or other she must have found out about Chris going to marry Louise, although there'd been no public announcement. Bert Harrington didn't even know Chris. Lisa kept her own counsel. I actually suggested getting rid of the baby for her – thought it might be the only way to avoid an open family scandal. God knows I didn't want to do it. I don't go in for that sort of thing, Sally, whatever you may think of me. But I do drink too much. Chris has helped me there. That's why I've tried to help him. It was a balls-up I made once when I was drunk that decided me to change my name. Or rather to drop the Hall. Chris helped me through that one. We've all got our weak spots. I've been lucky. He hasn't.'

Ralph paused for a while, but Sally said nothing.

'All right,' he said. 'I'll hurry up and you'll get your knockout dose of oblivion. Lisa said she didn't want me to get rid of the baby for her. If anyone was to do the job it ought to be Chris. If it really was his kid then I felt bound to agree, but I didn't say so. I begged her to keep quiet for a while so we could discuss what was best to do. She said she'd lie low if I'd send Chris to see her. I didn't fancy that very much, but couldn't see how to avoid it. If he didn't go to see her she'd come out and look for him. She knew her

213

way about those boats like a cat in the dark. I routed out Chris – he was skulking in his cabin most of the time, writing up some of his research results and composing poems to Louise – and told him about Lisa. I didn't like his reaction at all. He went quite quiet, an ominous sign. And when he talked it was with that sort of cold craziness that had preceded an earlier attack that I'd seen him through. I begged him to take no hasty action – we'd have to stall with Lisa until we could decide what best to do.'

Stall it off, thought Sally; yes, that's what Ralph would always do. Try to stall it off, take no action until it's too late. But even as she thought this, another voice came into her mind. That's not fair, said the other voice, and it seemed as if it held the tones of her uncle; that's not fair. Ralph did take quick action. He acted to save your life, and he was not too late. She shifted in her chair and gave a little moan. Then she said to Ralph: 'Please go on.'

'He said he'd decided exactly what to do,' continued Ralph. 'He didn't say whether or not he was responsible for Lisa's condition, but he said he'd get rid of the child for her and keep her there in his own cabin until we got to Southampton. He'd got a big cabin and he said he'd be able to keep the stewardess out of the way. Nobody else need know. He'd manage Lisa all right, and he'd get her ashore somehow – said he'd make up some story about her having been taken ill after coming on to the boat at Tenerife. I asked what I was to tell her father and he said, "Leave it to me. Tell him you've got a friend on board who's dealing with it all." Yes, Sally, you may well look like that. I know exactly what you are thinking of me. Cowardly rat. That's it, isn't it? All right. I won't attempt to defend myself. Of course I ought to have gone to the

214

captain with the whole story. Do you think I haven't wished a thousand times since then that I had done just that? Cowardly rat. All right. Let's weigh the pros and cons. I knew Chris had this dark side to him. I didn't like the look of him at that moment and it was obvious that Lisa could be a threat to his future. And to that of my own sister, of whom I happened to be very fond in spite of everything, though I can hardly expect you to believe that. I didn't want her to marry Chris, for more reasons than one, but she wanted to, and I had faced it and accepted it. I tried to convince myself – wishful thinking no doubt – that they would in some way reform each other, Chris and Louise. I wanted to believe it was for the best that their marriage went through without a hitch. I wanted to believe that Chris could deal with Lisa and that everything would be all right. That was my weakness. Wishful thinking. Weakness, not evil, Sally. I had no ill will. I'd nothing against Lisa. I'd nothing against Chris. I had absolutely no motive of ill will against anybody. But of course I can hardly expect you to believe that.'

Again Sally shifted in her chair. Her eyes were fixed on the vivid colours of the picture that hung over the mantelpiece – a view of a ship leaving Table Bay, the whole canvas ablaze with southern sunshine.

'I do believe you,' she said in a flat voice. 'I believe everything you say.'

'Thank you,' said Ralph equally flatly. Then he continued with more feeling: 'Now it's your turn. That's the last I saw of Lisa, when I told her I'd send for Chris. When I asked him later on how she was he said he was looking after her. He told Bert the same. When Bert wrote to me months later I wrote back the truth – the truth as Chris

215

had told me – that Lisa had simply disappeared. Not the truth as I had begun to suspect it. Not the truth that you are now going to tell me. Aren't you, Sally?' He leaned forward. 'You are now going to tell me exactly what you know. You are going to confirm my suspicion that Christian murdered Lisa.'

Sally withdrew her eyes from the sunlit scene in the picture and looked at Ralph. 'Not murder,' she whispered. 'Please, not murder. He did an abortion, and it went wrong, and she died. He didn't murder her.'

'It was murder,' said Ralph. 'There was no abortion. It was murder. You must face it, Sally. Now tell me. Tell me exactly what you saw on that boat. Slowly. Take your time. Forget Chris. Forget me. Forget everything except that you are looking at the truth. Looking at the truth in order to heal yourself. The healing truth. You are talking to a doctor of the mind and this doctor of the mind is helping you to see the healing truth – the healing truth . . .'

'Yes, yes, I know,' said Sally. She looked away from Ralph and back to the picture again, and began to talk in a low expressionless voice as if in a hypnotic trance. 'I came out of the cabin and I clung to the rail because the ship was rolling so badly. The door of the bathroom was shut, but the ship gave a great roll over, and the bolt slipped and the door burst open, and I saw a tall man, dark-haired and dark-skinned, with a thin white scar showing under his left eye . . .'

Her voice tailed off.

'The residue of an accident in childhood,' murmured Raph. 'Later he got glasses made that hid the mark.'

'He was standing on the ledge in the curve of the ship's

bows,' went on Sally, 'bending over so that his head did not touch the ceiling, and he had his arms round a woman. She was half through the porthole. I only saw the lower half . . .'

Again her voice faded.

'What did you see?'

'I saw a red skirt, crumpled up,' said Sally. 'I saw legs in light-coloured stockings. I saw black patent leather shoes.'

She stopped again.

'The legs,' said Ralph. 'How do the legs look? Are they hanging limply?'

Sally stared at him, then she stared at the picture, then back at Ralph again. 'Of course they are hanging limply.' she muttered at last. 'They must be. She is dead.'

'The red skirt, the light stockings, the black shoes, said Ralph in a low and urgent voice. 'You are looking at them – you are looking at them now – you are on a ship, the ship is tossing, first one side, then the other. You are looking at the legs with the black shoes – looking at the legs – the ship is rolling, everything on the ship is rolling too – the legs – the legs under the red skirt and the feet in the black shoes – are they moving? Do you see them move?'

Sally gave a little cry and covered her face with her hands. 'No, no,' she whispered. 'The legs don't move She's dead. She's dead, dead, dead, dead . . .'

Her voice died away. The hands covering her face began to tremble, then her shoulders began to shake, then she was shuddering all over, twisting around in the chair and violently shuddering. After a moment or two of this, while Ralph watched her closely, she gave a loud scream, jumped to her feet and began to scream and scream.

'No! No! She's not dead!' she cried, beating her fists against her eyes as if she would stop their seeing. 'Her legs are moving – it's not the ship's roll – they're moving in different directions . . . she's kicking, she's kicking! She's kicking off a shoe! It's coming off! She's not dead! She's alive! She's alive!'

The screaming started again. 'Help! Help! She's going to be drowned alive!'

'That's it, I think,' muttered Dr Ralph Curtis reaching into his black bag for a hypodermic syringe.

Chapter Eighteen

ABOUT A COUPLE of weeks later, on a mild afternoon in early November, Sally told Uncle James that she felt well enough now to go for a walk. Her mother and her Aunt Gertrude began to protest, but James Davenant overruled them.

'We won't go far. I shan't let her overtire herself,' he said.

'Well, Sal,' he said when they were clear of the entrance gates to Weir House, 'where do you want to go? Up to the church and back?'

'I want to go to the weir,' she replied.

'Are you quite sure? You never used to like going to the weir as a child. I used to think you must be afraid of it, but I never realized why. Now I understand, of course.'

'I want to go to the weir,' said Sally again, taking his arm.

'If you really want to,' said Uncle James, 'but there's no need to force yourself, you know. Plenty of time to get over it all – no need to rush things. Like shell-shock. That's what it is. Like shell-shock. Takes time to get over it. That's what Dr Curtis said. Sensible sort of chap. Give her time, he said. Just let her take her time.'

Uncle James glanced at his niece as he mentioned

Ralph's name. Sally's face was pale and set, and she made no response. She waited until he had finished, and then she said: 'Please, uncle, I really do want to go to the weir.'

'All right, love,' he replied. 'Just as you say. We'll go to the weir.'

She said no more, and they walked in silence along the gravel path, which was bordered by hedges of browning hawthorn leaves and wrinkling crimson berries and late garlands of wild clematis. At the first sound of the rushing water Sally's grip on her uncle's arm tightened, and he looked at her anxiously. She was staring straight ahead, and he thought it wiser not to speak.

They came to the footbridge with its concrete walkway and high iron-sided walls. The sound of the torrent was almost deafening. Sally pulled her uncle to a halt and smiled at him.

'I'm all right!' she shouted. 'It doesn't worry me now. Look!' And she let go of his arm and leant her arms on the top of the wall and peered over into the tumbling, bubbling water.

James Davenant leant on the rail too, closely watching her every movement. Dr Curtis had said she'd be all right now, but that her mind had taken a terrible tossing, and she'd need lots of kindness and care. A pity, thought Uncle James, that she didn't seem in the least bit interested in Dr Curtis's kindness and care, but perhaps one day . . .

'Careful, Sal!'

It burst out of him; he could not help himself. Sally had stepped on to the lowest rung of the iron framework so that she could see better, and she was leaning far over the bridge, staring down on the rushing water. James Davenant caught hold of the back of the loose coat she was wearing. He could not help being anxious. He'd asked Dr Curtis point blank whether there was any fear of the girl doing any harm to herself, and the doctor had said he was sure there wasn't, that her mind was as sound as a bell and it was just the shock, the shock that needed getting over. James Davenant supposed the doctor knew what he was talking about. For himself, he was an old man, a much older man now than he had felt two weeks ago; he didn't like the look of the world, and he didn't feel he wanted to see what it would look like if this war ever came to an end, this war that had barely even begun. There were only two people in this world whom he really cared for, and one of them had disappointed him sorely. Not only was she determined to stick to a man who was all that James Davenant hated most, but she had failed badly in love towards her sister when that sister was in great need.

'She shouldn't have gone poking her nose in,' Rose had said over the telephone when Uncle James had told her what had happened to Sally.

He had been deeply hurt on Sally's behalf. As far as his own feelings went, there was no one left now who could really touch his heart, only this tall fair girl looking as wan and pale now as when he had first seen her, a sick frail child with nothing but a flash in the eyes to show that she'd got a character and a will. Of course, he knew what was wrong. It was not only shock. That was just a pretence. Dr Curtis hadn't actually said so, but Uncle James had his own instincts, they didn't lie. She'd really loved the bounder. That was what was wrong with her.

His two beautiful nieces, lovely girls who had never hurt a soul, why should this happen to them both? One of them loved a common crook and had taken leave of her own decency for his sake. And the other had loved a murderer and the discovery of it had nearly killed her. It was enough to make the angels weep. It was certainly enough to moisten the eyes of a fond and foolish old man, even if the spray from the rushing water had not been moistening them already. He wished he knew what would cure a broken heart. Time, of course. Time ended all, in the end. But in the beginning and in the middle? Well, he himself had not got much to give; only his love and his money. If Sally wanted them she could have them all. Just let her stay alive; just let her not give up hope, not think all men were swine.

'It's rather lovely!' shouted Sally, stepping down off the iron rung. 'I enjoyed that.'

Either the leaning over or the whip of the water had brought a little colour to her cheeks. James Davenant's intense anxiety began to ebb.

'Had enough?' he shouted back.

Sally nodded, took his arm, and turned him in the direction of the footpath that led back to Weir House.

'Now we can talk,' she said when they were beyond the sound of the torrent. 'I've been thinking, Uncle James, and I'd like to join one of the services.'

James Davenant felt a little twinge of relief and a little twinge of apprehension, both at the same time.

'The Women's Auxiliary Air Force?' he asked. 'Charles Brent is joining the RAF, you know.'

'Yes, I know. Good for Charlie. He'll make a smashing pilot.'

James Davenant sighed inwardly. There was nothing but calm friendliness in Sally's voice. But then, he had known that there was no sense in recommending this very open and decent and totally acceptable young Englishman to Sally. If ever she loved again, which of course she would now that she was over the hump, it would be someone out of the ordinary, someone unusually brainy, unusually gifted, unusually something or other. She might love a cripple or a blind man or an anarchist or a foreigner or even a man of another race, but whoever it was, it would not be anybody in the least like young Charlie. James Davenant could only pray that it would not be anyone like that damned Boer doctor either.

'I had thought of the Air Force,' continued Sally, 'but now I've decided against it. I had to go and look at the weir before I made up my mind.'

'So you've made up your mind,' said Uncle James. 'May I be so bold as to ask which of the women's services is to be honoured by the presence of Miss Sally Livingstone?'

'The navy, of course,' said Sally pressing his arm. 'How could I possibly want to join anything but the navy?'

'You realize that you'll probably never go to sea?'

'That can't be helped.'

'And that if by chance you do, you'll only be seasick?'

'Then I'll have to put up with it, won't I? As Mother said, Nelson was seasick.'

'I can't imagine what your mother is going to say.'

Uncle James pretended to sound very serious and concerned. Inwardly he was rejoicing. She'll be all right, he was saying to himself; trust young Sal. She's kicked it all behind, and she's going to start again.

'I know exactly what Mother is going to say, and so do you,' said Sally. 'She's going to be thrilled to bits at being able to boast of her daughter in the Wrens to all her friends, and she always did say I looked best in navy-blue.'

'This calls for a little celebration,' said Uncle James. 'We'll have to see what your Aunt Gertrude has got in the larder.'

'Don't forget we're on food rationing now.'

'Food may be rationed, but spirits, never!'

Sally laughed. It was not a very loud laugh, but there was genuine merriment in it. 'Which sort do you mean, Uncle?' she asked. 'The bottled sort? Or the intangibles?'